ABOUT THIS BOOK

Welcome to Havenwood Falls, a small town in the majestic mountains of Colorado. A town where legacies began centuries ago, bloodlines run deep, and dark secrets abound. A town where nobody is what you think, where truths pose as lies, and where myths blend with reality. A place where everyone has a story. Including the high schoolers. This is only but one . . .

Miranda Saunders has spent her sixteen years playing by the rules. She's known for her impeccable style, good grades, and overall positive influence in Havenwood Falls. But in the vampire community, she's an oddity. Born a vampire, from a situation deemed impossible, Miranda's origins are an enigma to everyone. When a photo surfaces that brings up questions about her long lost father, she is determined to find the answers. That search lands her directly in the path of trouble—fellow vampire Kai Reynolds.

Having recently graduated from Havenwood Falls High, Kai is tired of being told how to behave. Ready to break out of the mold he's been cast in by his parents and the town's supernatural leaders, he becomes a prospect for the SIN motorcycle club—something his parents loathe.

But when he catches Miranda snooping around the clubhouse, he has to choose: turn her in and prove his loyalty to the club, or help her find the answers she's looking for. If they work together, they're both taking risks far more dangerous than they understand. And the mystery surrounding Miranda's father is only the beginning.

BLOOD & IRON

A HAVENWOOD FALLS HIGH NOVELLA

AMY HALE

Best Wishes!
xoxo,
Amy Hale

HAVENWOOD FALLS HIGH BOOKS

More books releasing on a monthly basis.

Stay up to date at www.HavenwoodFalls.com

Subscribe to our reader group and receive free stories and more!

ALSO BY AMY HALE

Ulterior Motives

THE SHADOWS TRILOGY
Shadows of Jane
Shadows of Deception
Shadows of Deliverance
Overshadowed (A Shadows Trilogy Novella)

Catching Whitney

Letters From Jayson

HAVENWOOD FALLS HIGH
Somewhere Within

HAVENWOOD FALLS
Flames Among the Frost

To my husband John, for always encouraging me to dream big and think outside of the box. And for all the great trips on our motorcycle. I love and adore you.

CHAPTER 1

A bell rang. The loud clanging resonated from somewhere nearby. I was certain it was a familiar sound, yet at that moment, it seemed foreign. I couldn't register the meaning, only that it was annoying, and I wanted it to stop. I closed my eyes and rubbed my temples.

"What's wrong with you?" a grating male voice spoke near my ear.

I snapped to attention. "What?" I turned to find myself uncomfortably close to Gary Smithson, one of our notorious school bullies. His dark eyes stared back into mine. I placed a hand on his chest and pushed him away. "Nothing. I'm fine."

"You don't look fine. Are you on drugs or something?" He smirked, and I knew he'd just *love* to spread that specific piece of gossip around school.

"No, moron. I'm not on drugs. I have a headache. Now go away before I tell the entire school that you still sleep with a night light."

His eyes grew wide. "What? How . . ." He looked around and ran a hand over his brown buzz-cut hair. "You're suck a freak."

Then he strolled away, his stocky build shifting side to side as he pretended I hadn't just nailed his fear of the dark, which was common knowledge in vampire circles, or more precisely due to the vampires in those circles.

I sat at my desk a moment longer as the classroom continued to empty. I'd done it again. For the past several weeks I'd been having involuntary moments where my consciousness seemed to check out, like my body was present but my mind was elsewhere. Each time I found myself mentally transported, often surrounded by mist or fog, and I was always looking for something . . . or someone. I never found whatever it was, and it always left me feeling empty. I also woke from this odd trance with a headache.

I gathered my books and made my way to my locker, willing my head to clear before I had to face the rest of the day.

My best friend Zoey reached my locker about the same time I did. "I'm so glad it's Friday and only a half day. I'm already tired of this school year," she moaned.

I chuckled. "It's barely been a week."

"I know. I'm just over it already," she grumbled.

"One day you'll look back and wonder how it all went by so fast." I repeated the words I'd heard adults say dozens of times.

She rolled her eyes. "Hey, I've gotta help my dad at the shop for a little while after I leave here, but then I'm free if you wanted to watch a movie at my house or something." Her mood brightened significantly at the subject change.

"Uh, yeah. Sure." I dug through my purse, looking for my house keys.

"Are you okay, Miranda? You've seemed kinda distracted lately. And you look tired."

"Do I?" I glanced at myself in my locker mirror. I did look a little tired, although only those closest to me would have really noticed it. My shiny long blond hair was still perfectly in place. My makeup was flawless and accented my features impeccably. Looking amazing was just one of the perks of being a vampire. My eyes, though . . . the gold flecks that were scattered within the dark irises were usually luminous. Now they seemed dull and joyless.

"Have you been sleeping okay?" She placed a hand on my arm.

"Mostly. I seem to just randomly zone out a lot. And I've been having some strange dreams. Like I'm chasing something or being chased. For some reason, I've had a lot of anxiety off and on. It hits at weird times. I can't seem to shake it." It sounds odd, vampires sleeping, but my mom and I, we're not your average Gothic vampires. Truth be told, we're not average in any way.

I hadn't told anyone about the dreams, the anxiety, or the trances, but Zoey was my confidante. I could tell her anything. She knew my darkest secrets, like the fact that I was a vampire. And I knew hers, such as her being a dragon shifter. Those were the kinds of things you took to your grave when roughly half the population in your town was human.

"Want to talk about it?" She glanced at her watch, and I knew she needed to get to her dad's shop.

"We can later. I'll meet you at the store after I've dropped some stuff off at home." I gave her a quick hug.

"Great, see you in a bit." She dashed down the hall and out the front doors of the school.

I loaded my backpack with the books I needed to take home and slung it over my shoulder. It was a relatively nice day, and I was glad I'd left my old car at home. It hadn't been running particularly well, and I enjoyed walking, when the weather was nice anyway. The exercise gave me time to think, and this was a day I needed it more than ever.

I mulled over various issues as I walked, trying to decide which one might be the cause of the unsettled feelings I'd been fighting. I'd just celebrated my seventeenth birthday, but it wasn't a major milestone like eighteen or twenty-one. It didn't have the feeling of big changes and responsibility that I assumed would come with those ages. I hadn't seen a lot of my mother lately, but I assumed that was due to a heavy workload. Being a marketing analyst could be demanding work. Most of the time, she worked remotely, but now and then she had to travel to the main headquarters in Denver. I didn't even know what her company sold. It had something to do with computers or something. Whatever it was, it paid the bills. It was just her and me, and Mom worked hard to provide for us. I had no siblings, and I didn't even know who my father was. Mom didn't talk about him.

Nothing I thought of fit. I couldn't describe the feeling other than to say it felt like I'd lost something important. And that I only had so much time to find it before it was gone from me forever. It was ominous and frightening. Despite what the movies said, Gothic vampires couldn't see into the future or read minds. At least, I'd never met any that could. And although I wasn't a normal Gothic vampire, I still didn't think visions or trances were something I should be experiencing. It felt . . . wrong. So I'd been left with this void I didn't know how to fill, and disturbing episodes I couldn't explain.

I unlocked the door to my house and put my backpack on the kitchen table. I scribbled out a note for Mom letting her know I'd be with Zoey the rest of the day, then I locked back up and walked toward the town square and Simple Treasures Pawn Shop. I hadn't quite made it to Eighth Street when I heard a noise from behind me that sounded like thunder. I felt it as well. The ground vibrated beneath my feet, and before I could even turn around, my senses were telling me to be alert and careful. I looked back just in time to see three large men on motorcycles roar past me. They were wearing leather cuts with the Swords of the Infernal Night logo on them. SIN was their acronym, and it seemed to fit them to a tee. While they appeared to be ordinary bikers, something about them gave off a vibe that they were anything but. That ominous feeling intensified, and I was anxious to get to the pawn shop.

I reached the store and walked in to find Zoey dusting a shelf loaded down with various old junk. None of it looked very valuable on the surface, and I couldn't see why anyone would want to buy it. There were belt buckles, military patches, medals, watches, small trinket boxes . . . all of it appeared beat up and dull. I assumed they held some kind of historical value, so maybe that was the attraction.

"What's all this junk?" I asked as Zoey lifted a small metal box.

She quirked one eyebrow up at me. "Junk? It's not junk. It's . . ." She waved her hand over it, as if that would somehow explain the purpose of the items before her. "It's . . . sentimental history."

"To who?" I crossed my arms. "The people that should care about it have pawned it."

Zoey opened her mouth, then shut it again. "Good point."

I laughed and nudged her side with my fist. Just being with her lifted my spirits. "How long do you work today?"

"Not much longer. I have to finish this shelf, then Dad said I had the rest of the afternoon free as long as nothing else came up. What kind of movie should we watch?" She pushed her raven black hair behind one ear, revealing some of the mother-of-pearl strands that ran through her tresses. Her hair was gorgeous, although she thought it was odd. I'd often told her it was a perfect accent to her stunning blue-gray eyes, but again she disagreed.

"Something funny." I didn't need anything scary or with major drama.

She glanced at me sideways as she continued to dust the shelf. "What? No campy slasher film? Blood and gore?" She turned to me. "Are you afraid it'll make you hungry?"

"No!" I nudged her again. "You know I'm not that kind of vampire."

"So if they were slaughtering woodland animals, you'd get hungry?"

I glared at her. "How do you like your humans? In barbecue sauce?"

Zoey laughed. "Sorry. You know I gotta tease you now and then." She dropped her rag on the counter and turned to face me. "Okay, well, what's the plan?"

"A funny movie. Or we could just hang out around town. See if there's anything new at Callie's . . . something like that."

Zoey shrugged as she picked up the rag once more and wiped down the last belt buckle on the shelf. "Sure. Any of that's better than doing nothing."

"Well," I sighed with dramatic flair, "I'm glad hanging out with me ranks just above 'doing nothing.'"

She put her hands on her hips. "Don't go all diva on me. You know what I meant."

I smiled. Someone in the hallway at school had once loudly called me a diva because I wouldn't hang out with her. While I was particular about my clothes, food, and who I spent time with, I was far from a diva. I was just very discerning where my tastes were concerned. That, and I wasn't your average vampire, so there were things about me I'd rather not divulge except to my closest friends. Spending time with me would ultimately bring those things to light. The biggest one was that I couldn't stomach human blood. I'd bring it back up every time. So instead, I fed on animal blood, which in my mind seemed cruel too, but it was better than starving to death. Human food was okay, and I'd eat it at times, but to really survive, vampires needed blood.

It was my turn to tease her. "Oh, you haven't seen a diva attitude yet. Just wait until I get my hands on Jordan. I'm gonna unleash the beast."

Zoey laughed. "Why?"

"Because I expected him to bring you one of those gorgeous flowered dresses from his vacation in Hawaii, and instead he brought you a T-shirt," I grumbled.

"Oh, you wouldn't. Besides, this is the first real vacation Jordan and his mom have taken since . . . ever. His dad wouldn't do things like that for his family. I'm glad they got to go. All I asked him to bring back for me was his gorgeous smile, tan buff bod, and photos from the island."

"I'm glad he went too, but still . . ." I crossed my arms in front of my chest. "I wanted to see you in one of those dresses like they always show people wearing on TV."

Zoey laughed. "Yeah, that wouldn't stand out on my super pale flesh at all."

"Hey, I'm the fashion maven of the two of us, and I'm telling you. It'd be perfect on you."

She waved me away as she put her cleaning supplies under a nearby cabinet. "Let me go see if Dad needs anything else. Maybe I can knock off now and we can grab lunch before we take off for the day."

I browsed around as she disappeared into the back room. The bell above the door rang, and I turned to see Zoey's grandfather, Lawrence Mills, slowly stroll into the room, his cane clicking on the hardwood floor as he moved. A young man with blond hair and an armload of boxes followed directly behind him, the pile teetering precariously every time he took a step. I recognized him as Glenn Williams when one of the boxes shifted and revealed his face. He used to go to school at Havenwood Falls High before he graduated last year.

"Miss Miranda. How are you today?" Mr. Mills smiled at me, but it never felt like he meant it. He had a tendency to creep me out.

"I'm well, thank you, Mr. Mills." I stood with my hands behind my back, hoping he didn't sense my discomfort.

"Glad to hear it." He turned to Glenn behind him. "You may put those on the counter."

Glenn did as he was told. Mr. Mills handed him some cash, and he scurried out of there as fast as he could. I didn't blame him. I didn't want to be around this cranky old dragon any longer than I had to, either.

"Please tell my son that I have some new items for inventory. He can keep what's valuable for the shop and toss the rest. I have an appointment, so I can't stay."

I nodded. "Happy to pass the message along, Mr. Mills."

"Thank you, girl." He turned and walked out of the store, not appearing to give me, or the business, a second thought.

Zoey and her dad, Tristan, came out of the back room a moment later.

"Was someone here?" Tristan glanced around. "I heard the bell, but I was on the phone."

"Yes, Mr. Mills dropped off those boxes for you. He said to keep the valuable stuff for the store and throw away the rest." I gestured to the boxes stacked on the glass countertop.

Tristan nodded. "Okay. Listen, girls, before you take off for the day, would you mind sifting through the boxes and let me know if there is anything special that catches your eye? I have a few more phone calls to make before I can take a lunch break."

"Sure, Dad," Zoey replied.

I nodded in agreement. I was happy to be helpful in any way I could.

~

AN HOUR LATER, we'd just finished rummaging through the fourth box and still had one box to go. My stomach was growling. Tristan had ordered pizza for us. And while I was happy to help eat it, I'd soon need real vampire nourishment. I'd have to run by Sanguine Elixirs to pick up my own special blend.

We nibbled on the pizza as we sifted through the last box. I was mindlessly examining a small photo album, enjoying all the old photographs and wondering what kind of life each person led. Most of them looked to be taken sometime in the sixties or seventies. But one photo stood out from the rest. I removed it from its sleeve and studied it closer.

"This is weird," I said as I continued to stare at the photograph in my hand.

"What is?" Zoey leaned over to see what I was looking at.

"That's my mom. It's many years ago, but that's her." My mom was a vampire as well, so she didn't age, but it was obvious by the clothing style that the photo had been taken sometime in the nineties—a few years before I was born, at least. Her blond hair was a tad longer than it was in its current shoulder-length cut. Unlike me, she had bright blue eyes. Her slim five-foot-seven-inch frame wore a tight pair of stonewashed jeans and a tank top with what I assumed was a band name. She stood with a group of tough-looking motorcycle guys, her arm around one man in particular. He was a few inches taller than her, with sandy blond hair and dark eyes. His build was lean and athletic. He had more of a southern rock look going on, with his leather pants and tattered cowboy hat.

The smile on Mom's face was huge. She looked carefree and truly happy. I wondered why I'd never seen that side of her before. Sure, she smiled and laughed at times, but even then, there was a solemn sadness underneath. I could sense it, and it made me ache for her. Her most common mood was stern, serious, and worried. I'd never understood it.

"The back has names written on it." Zoey took the photo from my hand, flipped it around, and quickly put it back in my grasp.

I squinted at the faded names. They'd been written in blue ink, and some weren't legible, but I could clearly make out my mom's name. *Sade Saunders*. The name next to hers read *Baxter Morrison*. I studied him closely, noting that something about him seemed familiar, but not quite putting my finger on what it was.

"Hey, girls. Find anything good?" Tristan walked back into the room with a stack of mail.

"Yeah, a few things." Zoey picked up a few forty-five records that had been bundled together in the first box. "This vinyl will probably be popular, now that records are kind of cool again."

Tristan frowned. "Records were never not cool. You kids just didn't understand the value in vinyl until recently."

Zoey smiled. "If you say so." She winked at me and leaned forward to whisper. "Never argue with old people about nostalgia."

"I heard that, young lady," Tristan said, never looking up from his pile of mail.

We both laughed, and I held up the photo. "Should we ask him?"

Zoey shrugged. "I guess it wouldn't hurt."

"Mr. Mills? Can I ask you something?"

He turned his head to look at me. "Only if you agree to call me Tristan. Mr. Mills is my father, and since I can't disown him, I'd at least like to distance myself from him in whatever way I can."

I nodded. "Sure, Tristan." It was weird saying that out loud, even though I'd always thought of him that way in my head for the same reasons.

I stood and took the photo to him. "Do you know any of these people? Did you live here then?"

He studied the photo and then glanced at me. His expression turned from humorous to concerned. "Where did you get this?"

"It was in one of the boxes." I pointed at the photo. "That's my mom."

He nodded. "It is indeed."

"Who are these other people?"

He cleared his throat. "This is a motorcycle club."

"How do you think my mom knows them?" I had a hard time envisioning my prim and proper mother hanging out with bikers. It just didn't seem like her thing. But the proof was there before my eyes.

"If you want to know more, you should ask your mother. This isn't my information to share." His voice was firm in that no-nonsense tone that I'd heard him use with Zoey many times. Asking him further questions would be futile.

"Okay, thank you. May I keep this picture?"

He was silent for a moment, then nodded. "Sure, but don't flash that around. Show your mom, and only your mom."

I nodded.

"I'm serious." He looked at me, and then at Zoey.

She nodded. "We understand, Dad. We'll be careful."

He handed the photo back to me, and I tucked it into the back pocket of my jeans.

Zoey slipped her arm through mine. "Can we go now, Dad? We have plans for the afternoon."

"Sure, go have fun." He waved us away and turned back to the paperwork in front of him.

Zoey and I stepped outside, and I pulled the photo from my back pocket.

"Whoa, maybe you should put that away until we get somewhere private. Dad acted like the very sight of it would start World War III or something." Zoey was trying to shield it from view.

"I will, I just want to look at it one more time." I shook my head. "There's something about that guy next to my mom. He looks familiar, but I can't figure out how I know him."

She leaned closer and inspected the photo with me once more. "I've never seen him, but it's funny. He kinda looks like you."

I froze. *He looks like me.* Or rather, I looked like him. "Zoey, I think Baxter Morrison is my father."

CHAPTER 2

*T*he afternoon with Zoey was fun. We watched an old movie and made cookies. I got home around five-thirty and finished what little homework I had for the weekend. After straightening up my room, I sat on my bed and stared at the old photo of my mother and her biker friends. This was not the woman I knew. The woman pictured looked truly happy. No worries or burdens dimmed the glow in her eyes. The smile was bright and full of hope. It made me wonder what had happened that changed her so much, outside of being the freak vampire that got pregnant. I was sure that put a dent in her social life.

Our kind didn't reproduce. We were created from what's already living. But somehow I was born. A miracle, my mom called it. I didn't feel like a miracle. I felt like there was something wrong with me. While we didn't talk about it in public, my mother had called me a mostenit, a Romanian word that meant "inherited." Against all odds, everything I was came from my mother and absentee father. So that was technically what we'd been calling my specific species of vampire. As far as I knew, I was the only one.

From what I understood, Mom went through the pregnancy alone, dealt with a lot of mocking and whispers from a majority of the vampire community, and spent most of her time taking online courses up until I was born. She didn't care about having a social life or what others thought of her. To our species of vampires, she was unnatural. To humans, she was just another sad pregnancy statistic. She didn't let any of that bother her, and she tried to raise me with the same outlook. We stuck close together as I grew up. She allowed me enough freedom to enjoy friends and activities, but at other times I was sure she was afraid to let me out of her sight. Especially as I got older. Now that I was in high school, she was very protective, and the most unhappy I'd ever seen her.

Mom's voice called for me from down the hall. "Miranda? Are you in there?"

I stood and put the photo back in my pocket. I needed to find the right time to ask her about it, but when would be tricky.

"Yeah, Mom, I'll be out in a moment." I took a deep breath and mentally prepared myself to walk through that door and pretend like everything was normal. I stepped into the hall and shut the door behind me. When I looked up, my mom was standing there, staring at me. She looked haunted.

"Are you okay?" I asked.

She swallowed and clasped her hands in front of her. "I will be." She paused to take a breath. "Let's have dinner, okay?"

I nodded. Something was up, so maybe this wasn't the best time to bring up her past.

I helped set the table, which to many would seem like a useless step for two vampires. But it was part of a comforting routine we'd established when I was little, before I knew we were vampires. And even though we didn't need to, we did occasionally still eat human food during dinner hours, just to try to feel like we fit in with normal people.

We enjoyed human food more than others of our kind. We were a lot like the moroi vampires in that way, as they also needed human food as much as blood. This was yet another thing that we were mocked for by the Gothic vampires when they found out. They didn't understand my mother's desire for me to have a few basic human experiences. She still remembered what it was like to be human, and she wanted me to know what that was like, too.

She'd made a small batch of pasta with marinara sauce. She usually mixed blood in with hers, but tonight I didn't feel much like eating pasta or anything else. Mom ate slowly, while I picked at mine.

"Mom?"

She swallowed a bite of her pasta. "Yes, sweetheart?"

"What's going on?"

She took a sip of her water and stared at her plate. "I've not been feeling well lately."

"What? What do you mean? Vampires don't get sick." I looked her over. Now that she mentioned it, I did notice the slight dark circles under her eyes, and what little color she did have was gone from her pallor.

"Well, I don't seem to be your average vampire." She sighed.

"So, did you go to a doctor?" Even to my ears that sounded nuts. Did doctors know how to examine vampires? My guess was no.

"I talked to Dr. Underwood and a few members of the Court, but none of them have ever heard of such a thing. Just like they'd never heard of our kind getting pregnant."

Panic caused my voice to raise an octave. "So what do we do?"

"I'm not sure yet, but I know it'll be okay. We'll figure it out." She gave me a reassuring smile. "We have some brilliant people in this town. Someone will know how to help."

I nodded, trying to trust that she was right. Witches, fae, dragons, demons, angels, gargoyles, ghosts—we had it all in Havenwood Falls. Someone should have some ideas.

"I know this is bad timing, but in light of what you just told me, I have to ask." I pushed down the ball of nerves that rose in my throat, and pulled the photo from my back pocket. I placed it on the table between us.

She picked it up, and for a moment, a small smile played at her lips. Then her eyes met mine. "Where did you get this?"

I watched her closely. "I found it when I was helping Zoey go through some stuff at the pawn shop."

"I see." She looked the photo over once more, then handed it back to me. "What did you want to know?"

"Baxter Morrison. Is he my father?"

She pressed her lips together and closed her eyes, as if the thought pained her. I hated that my question may have brought her any heartache, but I needed the answer.

"Yes," she stated flatly. "Baxter Morrison is your father."

"Who are all these other people?"

She shrugged. "Just some friends I used to hang out with when I was young and stupid." She stood up and moved to the cabinet, retrieving a wine glass, then her favorite merlot. Bringing them to the table, she sat back down. "I think I'll need this if you're going to ask more questions."

"I don't want to make you uncomfortable. I just feel it's time I knew the truth." I prayed she'd understand why it was so important to me, although to be honest, I wasn't totally sure of the reasons myself.

"I don't like talking about that part of my past. I made a lot of mistakes. Mistakes I pray you never make. And there are some questions I can't answer." She poured a small amount of wine into her glass and took a sip.

"Can't or won't?" I felt her usual shields starting to rise.

"Both." She took my hand in hers. "Miranda, please try to understand. I'm just trying to keep you safe."

"What does that mean?" I was getting annoyed, despite trying to keep my calm.

"It means that I will answer what I answer, and you are not to worry about the rest." Her tone was firm, and I knew that she was not going to budge on the topic.

"Fine." I huffed. "So are you going to tell me about the other people? Their names are on the back, although I can't make them all out. How did you know them?"

"They were just friends that I met through Baxter. I don't really talk to any of them anymore. That's all you need to know." She sat back in her chair and took another sip of wine.

"Okay then. Where is Baxter now?" She didn't appear to want to refer to him as my father, so I'd go along with it. I didn't mind calling him by his name.

"I honestly have no idea, Miranda. He left town after he found out I was pregnant with you, and I haven't spoken to him since." Exasperation showed on her features. I knew she wasn't going to entertain my questions much longer.

"I thought he was the love of your life? You used to talk about how great he was when I was little. Then you just stopped talking about him completely." I didn't understand why it was so terrible that I wanted to know about my father.

She groaned. "Miranda. I was trying to give you a father figure in your mind. I thought he was the love of my life too, but you're old enough to know the truth. He was a scumbag who didn't give a damn about you or me when it was all said and done. He screamed at me, accused me of cheating, and then walked out on us forever." She put her hands on the table. "Now, I'm done with this conversation. It's been a long day, I'm tired, and I want you to burn that photo, do you understand?"

"Burn it?" I couldn't believe what she was asking. "But it's the only photo I have of him. He may not be a good man, but this photo is the only connection I have."

She raised her voice. "And it's more than he deserves."

I flinched. She rarely yelled at me. I didn't normally give her reason to. Talking about Baxter must have really upset her.

This time in a softer tone, she said, "Sweetheart, it's less than you deserve."

Tears filled my eyes. I didn't know why this old photograph meant so much to me in that moment, but I couldn't bear to part with it. Not yet. "Mom, please. Let me keep it."

"Burn it, or I'll do it for you." She put her hand out, and I put the photo behind my back.

"Okay, fine. I'll do it. Just let me do it with Zoey, since she was with me when I found it." One of Mom's perfectly shaped eyebrows rose above her lovely blue eyes. It was the look she always gave me when she didn't understand my reasoning on something.

"It seems only fitting. Technically, it's her dad's property anyway, so I should give it back to him or get permission before I burn it."

She frowned. "Fine. Give it back, or get permission to destroy it. Either way, you are not to keep it. Understood?"

I nodded.

"Good." She leaned forward and kissed my forehead. "Now, I'm gonna go to bed. I have a long day tomorrow, and I'm not resting well. Maybe tonight will be better."

"Love you." I hugged her, reminding myself that no matter how mad I was, she was ill and I needed to take care of her in whatever way I could.

"I love you too, sweetheart." She walked through the kitchen and into the living area that led to her bedroom.

I worked to clear the table and load the dishwasher, all the while attempting to push down the guilt in my chest. I'd never disobeyed my mother. I'd always been the kid that followed the rules, stayed between the lines, and never questioned that the adults in charge knew what was best for me. But for the first time in my life, I was going to willfully disregard my mother's orders. I wasn't going to burn or give back the photo. And she'd be angry if she ever found out. But that horrible feeling I'd been fighting recently had to do with Baxter, and for whatever reason, I couldn't walk away from that so easily.

CHAPTER 3

$\mathcal{S}$aturday morning I got up early and went for a run. I'd worn my yoga pants, a T-shirt, and a light jacket to hold off the chill of the morning air. Fall was right around the corner, and in this Colorado box canyon, you felt it early. I'd put the photo of my parents in my jacket pocket, sure that if I left it at home, Mom would find it and destroy it herself.

After finishing my usual mile run, I sat alone in the gazebo in the town square to cool down. I'd been staring at the picture, just as I had been off and on since finding it, hoping somehow it would give me a clue as to why I felt so anxious and what connection Baxter had to it all. Despite Havenwood Falls being a small town, I didn't know everyone who lived there. Especially if they were supernatural. Some preferred to keep to themselves. Others only enjoyed the company of their own species. So it wasn't unusual for there to be people, especially adults, whom I wasn't acquainted with.

I felt the fog begin to roll around the edges of my mind. I couldn't stop it. My vision blurred, and everything surrounding me was muted and dull. I could just catch a glimpse of light in my peripherals, but no matter which way I turned, it escaped me. And there was a dull scream that sounded as if it were at the end of a very long tunnel. In my mind,

I was running toward it, trying to find the person screaming, but no matter how far I ran, I was no closer to them than when I started.

My head began to ache, and I found myself still sitting in the gazebo, photo in hand. I closed my eyes and took deep breaths as I worked to interpret what just happened. I was worried these zoned-out episodes were becoming more frequent.

A familiar male voice said, "Hey, there," and startled me from my thoughts. I dropped the picture, and it fluttered to the floor. Before I could grab it, slender fingers connected to a strong pale hand had already picked it up.

I held out my hand as I looked up at him. "I'd like that back, please."

Kai Reynolds stood in front of me, smiling like a cat that had caught a mouse. His dark brown hair was perfectly combed, except for the one lock that always seemed to fall onto his forehead. The lighter brown highlights were easy to spot now that the sun was out. His golden-brown eyes twinkled as he held the photo high above his head, not bothering to look at what he kept from me. "I'm sure you would like it back."

"Seriously, Kai. I'm not joking. Give it back." I stood, and while he was only about four inches taller than my five-foot-eight-inch stature, I still couldn't reach it. But I wasn't going to back down. He was a vampire as well, and though others were intimidated by his arrogance and muscular physique, I wasn't.

"My, we *are* touchy today." He handed the photo to me, but not before snatching it just beyond my grasp one last time to annoy me.

"Thank you." I sat back down and glanced at the photo to be sure it hadn't suffered any damage before putting it back in my pocket.

"I saw you sitting over here by yourself. You looked like you needed some company." He sat next to me and stretched his long legs out in front of him. When he leaned back against the bench, he casually draped an arm behind me.

"Do I look so pathetic that I'd want *your* company?" I couldn't help but poke the bear a bit. He deserved it.

"You look like you needed something amazing in your life, so here I am." He smiled at me, and I rolled my eyes.

"You're so full of yourself."

He shrugged. "I'm confident. There's a difference."

"No, not where you're concerned, there isn't." I stood up.

He grabbed my hand. "Wait, where are you going?"

"I'm leaving to make more room for your ego. I don't think we can both fit in here." I pulled my hand from his and walked down the short steps that led to the concrete path.

He chuckled behind me. "You always were a chicken."

I stopped and whirled around. "A chicken?"

He had the nerve to smirk at me. I'd always hated that smirk. In the three short years since he'd moved here, I'd often wanted to smack it off his smug face.

I stepped toward him again. "And why am I a chicken? Because I don't like being around a pompous elitist who discriminates against those who aren't like him?"

He was on his feet and in front of me in an instant. "Now, wait a minute. You don't know what you're talking about."

"Oh, really?" I placed my hands on my hips and looked him in the eye. "So why is it you never associate with anyone other than your small group of vampire friends? Why is it you don't attend parties you're invited to unless they are specific vampires? Why are you so opposed to interspecies relationships or even friendships, for that matter?"

He glared at me, but said nothing.

"Yeah, that's what I thought." I turned to walk away.

"You don't understand anything." His tone was low and angry.

I didn't give him the satisfaction of looking back to acknowledge his answer. I kept walking until I reached Coffee Haven and went inside. I ordered my usual white mocha and chose a table at the back of the shop. I needed to think, and my mind was muddled. My thoughts kept whirling between the odd trances, finding Baxter, and the irritating interaction with Kai a few minutes earlier. I didn't talk to him often, but when we did speak to each other, it always seemed to end in a verbal joust. One I didn't always win.

The bell over the door rang, and I looked up to see Zoey's aunt Jetta walk in. She was kind of known as the town bad girl, although if you really knew her, you learned that she was a great person. She'd been in some trouble in the past, but that wasn't all necessarily by choice. She'd run with the wrong crowd once upon a time. She did look the stereotypical bad girl, though. Short, spiky silver hair, multiple piercings and tattoos, and she wore tight clothing like she'd invented the look.

I kind of envied her free spirit. I've always worn the latest styles and was known for setting a few trends in our little town, but everyone expected a certain kind of behavior from me. It's all my own fault. Since I was little, I'd found myself working hard to please everyone. I was that poor little girl without a dad and with a mother who worked all the time. I'd heard the judgmental whispers about Mom and me from an early age. Later, when I learned the truth about myself, I discovered I was viewed as the odd vampire that defied the nature of our species. I battled both of those stereotypes with everything I had. I overshot it a bit. To the human world, I was this upstanding young citizen getting good grades and volunteering when I had time. To the supernatural world, I was still a freak of nature, but considered well-behaved, and I never stepped out of place. And while I did generally enjoy being viewed as a respectable young woman who set standards to be proud of, sometimes it all felt forced. I wanted to break loose now and then, but I feared doing so would only start the whispers of "I told you she was no good."

Jetta was a rocker by trade, so if she got rowdy and loud, no one batted an eye. It was just all part of who she was, on and off the stage.

She grabbed her coffee, saw me, and came over to sit down. "Hey, chick, how ya doing?"

"I'm good." I took another sip of my mocha. "How about you?"

"Same." She smiled and leaned forward with a conspiratorial whisper. "Conrad keeps asking me to pick a date for the wedding, but I'm enjoying making him sweat a little."

I laughed. "You are so bad."

She pointed a finger at me. "Hey, always keep a little mystery in your relationship. Give your man a reason to keep digging and learning about you. It keeps things interesting."

I shook my head. "Well, that would require a man first."

She took a sip of her coffee. "What about that Kai fella? I saw you two talking in the square a bit ago."

"Oh." I laughed nervously. "Oh ho no. He's not at all my type."

"Really? What type is he?" She smiled behind her cup.

I frowned a bit. "He's arrogant. Condescending. Elitist. Reckless. Bossy."

"Hot," she interjected.

"Well, yeah, but that's superficial," I amended.

"Maybe, but he might be good for you." She winked at me.

"You've got to be kidding me." I couldn't hide the disgust in my voice.

She shook her head. "I'm totally serious."

"Have you forgotten what he did to Zoey at the ball?" I couldn't believe she was suggesting I date Kai Reynolds, of all people.

"No, I haven't forgotten. But he was being pushed into those shenanigans by my father. You know how persuasive the almighty Lawrence Mills can be when he wants something. He didn't want Zoey dating a human, so he pushed Kai into trying to steal her away from Jordan. I don't hold it against Kai for doing what his elders told him to do, even if it was stupid."

"We can barely stand the sight of each other," I stated flatly.

"Hmmm . . . that's not what I witnessed in the gazebo," she said in a sing-song voice.

My eyes shot to hers. "Then you misread the situation."

"Oh, I don't know. I think I know sparks when I see them. I am marrying a lava dragon after all." She winked at me.

"Eventually," I retorted.

"You got me there, kiddo." Jetta reached across the table and took my hand. "Sometimes you have to take a chance in life to find what you're really looking for. What you need isn't always what you think it should be. Happiness rarely shows up in the package you pick out for yourself."

I felt sure Kai wasn't it, but her words did strike a chord on another matter. "Can I ask your help with something?"

"Sure." She sat back in her chair and twisted one of the skull rings that adorned her fingers.

"I found this photo of my mother, from a long time ago. Do you know any of the other people?" I pulled the picture from my pocket and slid it across the table.

Jetta picked it up and studied it for a moment. "Wow. This was a while back."

I nodded. "Do you know anything about the people she's with? Or Baxter Morrison?"

Jetta lowered the photo. Her eyes were full of a sadness I felt deep within. "Oh, honey. This isn't a road you want to go down."

I felt tears prick the corners of my eyes. "Why does everyone keep saying that? He's my father. I have a right to know about him."

"I understand, Miranda, but this isn't the way to learn. These people . . ." She hesitated, like she was choosing her words carefully. "They aren't the kind of people you want to cross."

"Are they murderers or something? Was my dad a criminal?" Even if I hated the answer, I needed to know.

"It's not as simple as that. The situation with them . . . it's very complicated." She handed the photo back to me. "What does your mom say?"

"Nothing. She tells me nothing." I wiped away angry tears. "She wants me to forget about all of this and burn the picture."

"Well, I can't say I blame her. She's just trying to protect you. If I had a daughter, I'd do the same." Jetta closed her eyes briefly. "I can tell you that he hasn't been back in town since he left in 2001. No one has heard from him or contacted him, and he's never coming back."

"Did you know him?" I couldn't hide the small hint of hope in my voice.

"Not very well. I'd only talked to him a couple of times." Jetta downed the last of her coffee. "He was a wild one. He liked to party.

He had a reputation of sorts. He was good at getting into trouble. But that's really all I should say." She took a deep breath, then exhaled. "Now, if you need me, you call me anytime, sweetie, but be careful with this." She tapped her finger on the picture still sitting on the table. "There are people in this photo that might not appreciate you digging into their business."

"Sure," I said, as I worked on finishing the last of my drink as well.

"Okay, I need to run. I've got rehearsal and errands before my show tonight. Are you good?"

I nodded and forced a smile. "I'm good."

"Aww, you're lying, but I appreciate the effort." She stood and kissed the top of my head. "You're a great girl. Don't let anyone change that, no matter what happens in your life. Stay true to what's in here." She poked her finger at my chest as she spoke. "Your heart will never steer you wrong."

"I will. Thanks."

She winked at me, grabbed her cup, and walked to the front of the shop.

Once again I was alone with my thoughts, left wondering what awful thing my parents had been so mixed up in that no one will talk about it. Jetta said to be true to myself. And that sometimes we had to take risks to find what we were looking for. I'd never really been a risk taker, but that was about to change. I wasn't a child anymore, and this aching in my soul would never cease until I had the answers I needed. I would have to be careful, but I would find out the truth.

CHAPTER 4

I only knew of one motorcycle club in town—the notorious SIN club. While there was no proof they were doing anything illegal, there had been whispers of nefarious activities for as long as the club had existed. I had only just started hearing the rumors in the last couple of years. The adults in town had been very careful about what information was passed on to the kids, but secrets tended to get around once you were in high school. We'd all heard talk about the club full of big scary guys with equally scary reputations. No one ever came out and accused them publicly, but the whispered rumors often connected them to various disappearances and other questionable activities. Some people claimed that SIN did the less-than-desirable deeds for the Court. Others had said they operated outside of the law when not in town. And there were those who believed that SIN did whatever they wanted because they were untouchable. Who really knew what was fact and fiction?

Was Baxter a member of SIN? It was hard to comprehend. Visualizing my mother hanging out with, let alone dating, a member of such a disreputable group seemed ludicrous. Yet the proof stared back at me right there in the photo—she was standing with a whole group of them. She'd said herself that it was when she was young and stupid. I didn't know if her reasons for not telling me were more for my safety or because she was ashamed of her past. Maybe it was a mixture of both.

I decided the only way I was going to learn more about Baxter was to learn more about SIN first. So my plan was to start at the beginning. Or rather, the only beginning I knew of anyway.

That evening I waited until my mom was asleep before I left the house. It hadn't taken me long to locate the clubhouse, since I'd heard it was right next to the Cerberus Delivery building.

The clubhouse turned out to be a red brick building with a thick wooden door guarding the entrance. Above it hung a sign with the logo for SIN. It was a sword-impaled skull with roses wrapped around the hilt. I sat outside of the building for about thirty minutes before I finally worked up the nerve to sneak inside.

Music could be heard filtering through the front door, so I made my way around back to see if there was another way inside. I found a back entrance, so I slipped through the door, which thankfully didn't squeak, and pressed my back against the wall. A wall that did not feel clean. I cringed and tried not to imagine what kind of nasty things I might be rubbing off on my new blouse. Music came from the opposite end of the hall, and the stench of cigarette smoke and alcohol was strong. I wrinkled my nose, determined I wouldn't let anything deter me from my mission. It was dark, apart from the glow of neon coming from somewhere near the front of the building. I assumed that must have been the main part of the clubhouse. The shadows would help me sneak around a bit, but also made it difficult, since I didn't know the layout of the club. I stopped and took some deep breaths, trying not to cough when the smells hit me stronger this time.

I listened carefully, trying to ascertain where all the voices were coming from. It was a little hard to tell over the music. I hoped that with any luck, they were all in the room with the neon and music, so I could snoop around a bit. I took a careful step to the side, wanting to dislodge myself from whatever nasty substance had me temporarily stuck to the wall, but worried any bigger movements would alert someone to my presence.

My eyes were adjusting to what little light there was, and I could see several doors on either side of me.

I took several more cautious steps until I was almost at the door leading to the noisy room. I thought it might be good to know what I was facing. I peeked around the door to see several burly men and a few women in a very large room. I quickly pulled back. My mind started to race, and the hairs on the back of my neck felt as if they were standing on end. *What am I doing? I don't even know what I'm looking for. This may not be the best idea after all. I'm in way over my head, and I should leave while I can.* Nerves caused my stomach to do somersaults. I listened to shouts and laughter as I took one step backward to disappear back into the hallway.

The sound of several bottles tipping over and spinning on the hardwood floor suddenly echoed through the building. Despite the music, I was sure I'd just sent an alarm up to the entire clubhouse. I froze. I'd kicked the stupid bottles. That was it. I was dead.

I held my breath as I heard the rustling of bodies near the doorway. Then a hand clasped over my mouth, and someone pulled me deeper into the hall. I struggled to get free, but whoever had me was very strong. Much stronger than me.

He pulled me up against him and hissed into my ear. "Shut up and stay still if you want to live."

I stopped moving, hoping I was making the right decision by obeying his commands.

He pulled me with him as he moved closer to the hall doorway, then leaned out slightly, keeping me against him but out of sight. "Sorry, guys. I just tripped over some bottles."

Kai? Why is Kai here?

Mumbles and groans came from the main room, with one gruff shout of "Clean that crap up." Then it sounded as if they resumed their previous activities.

Kai pulled me back down the hall to the end, and out the back exit, keeping his hand over my mouth the entire time. Once outside he shoved me away from him.

"What in the . . ." He clenched his fists above his head in what appeared to be frustration. "Are you out of your mind?"

I had just been asking myself the same thing, but I ignored his question for the moment. "Don't you ever grab me like that again. Do you understand?"

I brushed off my sleeves and jeans, hoping that if there was any grime from the building still on me, I could sweep it away.

"Miranda." He stepped closer, his tone giving away his irritation. "I just saved your neck. How about a little gratitude?"

"Saved my neck?" I knew he was right, although I wasn't sure how he'd done it. And I didn't want to give him credit for anything that might give him a hero complex.

"Yes. If they had found you in there . . ." He shook his head. "It could have been really bad."

He ran his hands through his hair, and I noticed they were shaking. He was truly rattled. I'd never seen Kai Reynolds upset by anything.

"Are you okay?" It felt weird even asking him such a question. I shouldn't care. I didn't care, I told myself.

"I'm fine." He put his hands in his jeans pockets. "Let's get out of here. We need to talk somewhere less likely to get us in trouble."

I nodded. "Sure."

I would normally argue with him just for the chance to put him in his place, but seeing Kai so concerned caused me more anxiety. It was eerie to see him that way.

I followed him around the building until we reached a motorcycle that looked brand new.

He pulled an odd-looking key out of his pocket just before throwing his leg over the seat. Kai looked back at me. "Hop on."

"What?" I knew nothing about motorcycles, except that they were dangerous if you didn't know what you were doing. I'd never seen Kai on one.

He sighed, then spoke slowly. "Get. On."

"Are you nuts?" I looked around. "I'm not getting on that death machine with you. We were lucky enough to get out of the clubhouse, but stealing one of their motorcycles is just stupid."

"*You* were lucky to get out. And I'm not stealing anything. This is my bike."

I felt my mouth pop open. "When did you get a motorcycle?"

"I bought it late last year when the 2018 Fat Boys rolled off the assembly line." He smiled and rubbed a hand over the metallic blue tank with pride.

"Fat boy?" I raised an eyebrow.

"This is a Harley Davidson Fat Boy."

"Oh, I guess it's obvious I know nothing about motorcycles." I put my hands on my hips.

"It is, but you are part of a large group, so don't feel bad about it." He smirked at me in that condescending way that always made me want to throw something at him.

"I don't feel bad about it." I huffed. "I don't care about motorcycles, so there's no need for me to have any knowledge on the subject."

"Well, lucky for you, knowledge isn't required to be a passenger. So quit stalling. Get your butt on this seat so we can get out of here."

"Wow, you are such a jerk." I crossed my arms. "Do you even know how to drive that thing?"

"I do." He didn't offer any further explanation.

"Fine." I climbed on behind him, letting my feet rest on the pegs behind his legs.

"What do I hold on to?" I tried to sit upright and pushed myself as far away from him as I could without sliding off the back of the seat.

"Me. You hold on to me."

That did not appeal to me at all. I pinched a bit of fabric from his shirt between my forefinger and thumb on each hand.

"I'm not gonna bite you, Miranda. Not unless you ask me to."

I smacked his shoulder.

He chuckled. "You will need to wrap your arms around me and scoot closer if you don't want to fly off the back and land on your butt.

I groaned.

"Fine. Have it your way." He started the bike and revved the engine a couple of times before pulling into the street.

I immediately wrapped my arms around his chest and pressed myself against his back. It felt like we'd gone from zero to a hundred miles an hour in seconds.

I yelled over the rumble of the engine. "Slow down! You're going too fast!"

"Calm down. I'm doing the speed limit." He shook his head at me.

I gripped him tighter and closed my eyes. I didn't want to see whatever it was that we'd eventually run into. Another weird quirk about me: I could heal myself, but it was a slower process than for most vampires. And I didn't like pain, so I preferred to avoid it whenever possible.

I felt the wind whipping my hair around my face as we sped down the road. If I was being totally honest, it was a tad exhilarating. Not that I was going to say any such thing in front of Kai. He'd just spout something conceited and pat himself on the back.

We'd only been moving a few minutes when I felt the bike slow. I cracked open one eye to see we were nearing Danzan Lake. He pulled off the road and parked in a patch of grass.

"Why are we here?" I looked around at the peaceful setting. The moonlight reflected off the still water and made the lake resemble a large sheet of glass. Trees dotted the shoreline on the opposite side, and I could hear crickets everywhere.

"I figured this was a safe place to talk." He sat still for a moment. "Um . . . you can let go now."

I looked down to realize I was still clinging to him. "Oh. Sorry."

I released my grip and slid off the seat, happy to have my feet on solid ground again.

He stood and dismounted the bike, then walked to the edge of the water. I followed, and once at his side, he turned to face me.

"What were you doing sneaking into SIN tonight?" His frown and eyebrows angled severely downward.

"I . . . wait. You tell me why you were there first." I wasn't sure I wanted to share the news of my father with him. I expected him to mock my existence and lack of a proper two-pure-vampire-parent household.

"No, I asked you first. Why were you there, Miranda? If anyone had caught you, the consequences would have been serious. Why would you put yourself in danger like that?" He sounded angry.

"I have my reasons, and they are none of your business." If he wanted to be angry, I could be angry, too. "What were you doing there? You were in just as much danger." I poked at his chest.

"No, I wasn't." He crossed his arms.

"Oh, really? And what makes you so special that a bunch of badass bikers wouldn't beat the crap out you for being in their clubhouse?"

"Well, I'm a member, for one." He smirked at me again.

"What?" My voice did that high-pitched squeaky thing I hated when I was caught off guard.

"Okay, not a member yet. But I'm a prospect."

"And why would you do this?" I was now the one trying to find logic in *his* actions.

"Because I want to. My buddy Jack Peters is prospecting soon. He lives there since his dad is president of the club, so it's fun to hang out with him." He paused. "And that's all I can tell you. We aren't allowed to talk about the club." He put his hands on my shoulders. "Now, back to the question you keep trying to avoid. Why where you there?"

I didn't know what to tell him. The truth would be easiest, but Kai was a snob. His parents had brought him to Havenwood Falls to rub elbows with the rest of the rich people and turn him into one of the town elitists.

"Now, out with it." He looked into my eyes, and for a moment, I didn't feel annoyance toward him. He truly seemed concerned.

"I can't talk about it, Kai. It's personal." As hard as I tried, I couldn't keep the tremble out of my voice. All the emotions from the night had started to crash in on me. I closed my eyes and took a deep breath while I worked to steady myself.

He put one finger under my chin and tilted my face up so his eyes could search mine. "I know you think I'm a jerk. And sometimes I am. But I would never do anything to purposely hurt you. Despite the opinion you've formed, without getting to know me, I might add, you can trust me." He paused and waited for me to answer, but I couldn't move words past the lump in my throat. He put his hands by his sides. "Maybe I can help you."

It was then that it struck me. Maybe he actually could help. He was welcome among the members of SIN.

"I was looking for information . . . about my father." I tried not to outwardly cringe while I watched his expression. I was expecting disgust at the mention of my absentee father. Instead he looked confused.

He stepped back and put his hands on his hips. "Why would you think the club would have information on your dad?"

"Because of this." I pulled the worn photo out of my pocket and passed it to him.

He looked at the picture. "Is that your mom?"

I nodded.

He continued to study the photo. "You assume one of these bikers is your dad?"

"No, I didn't assume anything. My mother confirmed it. The man next to her, Baxter Morrison, is my biological father."

He handed the photo back to me. "Wow. That's a lot to take in."

"Yeah, it is."

"So you think he was a member of SIN, and you hoped to find something about him by snooping around the clubhouse." He spoke it as a statement, not a question.

"Something like that."

"These are not the kind of people you mess with. Or steal from. The leaders are hellhounds, for crying out loud. Have you ever seen a hellhound?"

I shook my head. "Not as far as I know."

He scoffed. "Oh, believe me. You'd know."

"I have to do something, Kai. I can't explain it, but I need to find my father. It's important." I once again felt the tears threatening to fall. But I'd rather swallow my tongue than cry in front of Kai Reynolds.

"Miranda." He pinched the bridge of his nose. "This is a suicide mission."

"Forget it. Just take me home." I stomped back to the bike and waited for him to follow.

His voice was directly behind me in seconds. "You're gonna do it anyway, aren't you? No matter what I say, you're gonna poke around and get yourself hurt."

I didn't answer.

"I'm so gonna regret this," he muttered.

I turned to face him. "Regret what?"

"I'm going to save you from yourself. I'm going to help you get the information you're looking for."

"I don't think—"

He cut me off with a wave of his hand. "On one condition."

"What would that be?" I eyed him with suspicion.

"You have to promise to let me handle this. And if we don't find anything, you drop it."

I shook my head. "No way. You have no stake in this, so it doesn't matter to you if you find anything or not."

"No stake? If they find out I'm helping you, they could kick me out . . . or worse." He shook his head. "I'm putting my future on the line for you here. I promise to do my very best to find what you are looking for, but in return, you have to let me do this my way and not stir up trouble. You have to stay out of the way."

I thought on that for a moment. I might have to have him clarify what he meant by "stay out of the way." This was my father we were discussing, after all. But for the moment, I agreed. I did need his help. Tonight had been a close call, and I did not want to find myself face to face with a hellhound.

"Agreed, for now."

He sighed. "I guess I'll take what I can get."

CHAPTER 5

I didn't sleep well, and the following morning I had very little appetite. I sat at the breakfast table but had barely touched my usual morning smoothie. I found myself so preoccupied with the events of the previous evening that I almost jumped when my cell phone rang.

"Are you okay?" Mom's voice held concern.

"Yeah, I'm fine. Would you excuse me? I should take this." I pulled my phone from my pocket and walked down the hall to my bedroom. I quickly closed the door behind me and turned on my MP3 player in case Mom was attempting to listen in.

"Hello?"

"Miranda, it's Kai."

"Oh, hi. I didn't expect to hear from you so soon." I sat on my bed. My stomach was in knots.

"Well, I hadn't planned to call you this morning, but you need to know there's been a slight change of plans." His voice sounded odd, like he was nervous.

"A change? How?" I bit my lip.

"When I got back to the club last night, Liam Peters asked me where I'd gone. He's one of the founders of the club and the president.

33

One of the hellhounds you need to avoid." Now I knew the tone of his voice wasn't just in my head.

"And what did you tell him?"

"He saw me leave the club with you. He could smell you in the club. He knows you were there, Miranda."

"Oh, no." I gasped.

"I had to make something up on the fly to save both our butts. The only way this works is if you go along with it."

"Okay, so what's the plan?" I had a feeling things were going to go from bad to worse.

"I told him that you were my girlfriend."

"What?" I screeched.

"Hear me out." He sighed. "I told him that we'd been dating a few weeks, but that you thought I was lying to you about being at the club. You thought I might be cheating on you. You got jealous and were hanging around outside, trying to catch me in the act, or at least in a lie about being there. When I saw you, I took you home, we fought, made up, and now all is good. I assured him you won't be repeating that mistake again."

"And he believed that bull?" I stammered.

"He actually did, for the most part." Kai chuckled softly.

"I can't imagine why. And thanks for making me look like a jealous harpy." I thought that irritated me more than the girlfriend lie.

"Well, it didn't hurt that I told him who your mom was. He remembers her and Baxter. He figures like mother like daughter, I guess."

"I don't know if I should be insulted or flattered by that." I huffed.

"Probably both." He laughed again.

"This isn't funny, Kai!"

"Aw, come on. It's a little funny."

"It is not," I growled between clenched teeth.

"Well then, you are really not gonna like this part." I could almost hear that smug smirk of his.

"And what would that be?"

"We're gonna have to sell it. We have to make it public so he doesn't doubt any aspect of our story. And so he doesn't question if I bring you around now and then, or ask about Baxter."

"Um . . . absolutely not." I couldn't believe what I was hearing. There was no way I was pretending to date Kai Reynolds.

"Fine." His voice went hard. "Then enjoy watching your back for the next several years, while I skip town."

"Seriously?" He had to be exaggerating.

"Seriously. If they find out I lied . . . I don't know how bad the consequences could be. You don't cross SIN." He didn't sound like he was joking. And Jetta had said the same thing to me yesterday. We were in deep trouble, thanks to me.

"Ugh . . . crap on a cracker. Fine. I'll do it." I sighed, resigned to the fact that this was going to be a horrible experience.

"Crap on a cracker?" Kai laughed.

"Shut it. We make this the shortest relationship possible, got it?"

"I got it." He reverted back to sounding annoyed.

"So what now?" I wasn't sure I really wanted to know.

"I'm going on a run with the club later, but how about we do something tonight? We could grab dinner or see what's on the schedule at the Annex. Something so we are seen in public. I'll let you choose."

"Oh boy. Okay, I guess we could get dinner. We both need to eat anyway, so we might as well be at the same table and kill two birds with one stone."

"How logical." I swear I could hear that smirk again. He was mocking me. "I'll pick you up at six-thirty."

"Not on the death machine," I replied quickly.

He laughed and hung up on me.

"Ahhh," I moaned into the air. "He makes me so crazy sometimes."

THE DAY SEEMED to drag on, and I couldn't focus on any one thing. I was really nervous about my fake date with Kai. I knew it wouldn't take long for word to get around that we were together, which was both good and bad. Good for our particular purpose, but bad because I disliked the thought of my friends believing we were really dating. I couldn't tell anyone the truth, except maybe Zoey. She'd keep our secret, even though she wasn't Kai's biggest fan.

I dressed in my favorite jeans and a white long-sleeved top, with the addition of some silver jewelry and white boots. I pulled my hair back at the sides, allowing the rest to hang down my back.

At exactly six-thirty, I heard the rumble of Kai's motorcycle pulling into the driveway. I'd been sitting on the sofa, hoping to intercept his arrival. My mom had just walked in and heard the noise as well. I hadn't told her I was going on a date, let alone who it was with. I'd really wanted to sneak out before she had the chance to ask any questions, but Kai just screwed that all up. I was sure I'd end up killing him before this was all over with.

"Who's here? Are you expecting company?" Mom walked to the door and opened it.

Kai stood on the other side, his smile wide, and as usual, he was dressed impeccably. Even I had to admit he looked good in his black slacks and snug blue polo shirt. "Hello, Ms. Saunders. You're looking lovely, as always."

Mom smiled at him. "Why, thank you, Kai. That's very sweet of you to say." She stepped aside to allow him entrance.

Suck-up.

He turned to face me. "Hello, Miranda. You look beautiful."

He held out a small bouquet of daisies—my favorite. For a moment, I was speechless. He was really putting on quite a show to convince people we were dating, and we hadn't even left my house yet.

"Thank you. These are lovely." I held them awkwardly, unsure of what to do with them.

Mom came to the rescue. "Let me put those in water for you." She gave me a look that said *What is going on?*

"Thanks, Mom."

She stepped into the kitchen, and I turned my attention to Kai.

"Daisies?" I whispered, again trying to ensure Mom couldn't hear our conversation.

He stepped closer. "They're your favorite, right?"

I nodded. "Yes, but how did you know that?"

He shrugged. "I remembered hearing it somewhere. You probably told me at some point during school or something."

I raised one eyebrow. "I can't think of a single social situation that required my discussing my flower preferences."

He simply shrugged again. "Lucky guess then."

"Uh huh." I didn't believe him for a moment. I was sure he'd asked someone about that tidbit of knowledge. I guessed that was the sort of thing a boyfriend should know about his girlfriend, fake or otherwise, but that didn't mean I had to like it.

Mom reentered the room, and we quickly stepped apart. "So do you kids have plans for the evening?"

She was trying so hard not to ask the obvious question.

Kai didn't give me a chance to answer. "Miranda has agreed to a night out with me."

He flashed his perfect white teeth once more. I almost groaned out loud. He was too happy about all this and was overselling it. She'd get suspicious if he didn't tone it down.

"We're just gonna grab dinner and hang out for a bit. I won't be out too late."

She nodded. "All right then. You two have a good time."

Kai opened the front door for me, and I stepped through onto the front porch.

When the door shut behind him, I whirled to face him. I gestured to the motorcycle in the driveway behind me. "I told you not to pick me up on that thing."

"Yes, you did." There was that smirk, combined with his right eyebrow cocked at an arrogant angle. I was now convinced he did this just to irritate me.

I put my hands on my hips. "But you did anyway. Why?"

"Because that's my main mode of transportation at the moment. Besides, it's fun."

I rubbed my temples. "Only to crazy people."

"Call me what you like, but at least I know how to loosen up a bit."

I narrowed my eyes at him. "Are you calling me rigid?"

"I'm saying you're so terrified of relaxing and bending the rules that you never truly enjoy anything." And cue the smirk.

I released a very unladylike snort. "Let's go. The sooner we eat, the sooner this is over with."

I walked over to the bike, thankful I hadn't worn a skirt.

He threw one leg over the seat and settled in. I climbed on behind him and remembered that I had to hold on to him tightly to keep from sailing off the back like a cup left on the roof of someone's car.

"Could you maybe take things a little slower this time? It'd be great if my eyeballs weren't completely dried out by the time we got to the restaurant."

"Sure." He started the engine and pulled out of the drive.

I didn't have to grip him for dear life this time, so the ride was a little more enjoyable. I was able to watch as the modest little homes of our neighborhood gave way to the buildings in the town square. Soon we were driving out of town and picking up speed. I wrapped my arms around him tighter, willing myself to keep my eyes open and take in the view of the landscape.

The green of the blue spruce and pines was sprinkled among the quickly changing leaves of the sugar maple and sycamore trees, as well as the gold of the quivering aspens. The contrast was gorgeous. I could look to either side and see rocky outcroppings and peaks that stretched far past the clouds. Even at sixty miles an hour it was breathtaking. The air was so clear and crisp that I found myself wondering how people in crowded cities could stand to breathe. I'd never been outside of Havenwood Falls, but I'd heard awful stories about the air pollution in some of the bigger cities. Zoey had experienced a bit of it herself.

We pulled into the parking lot of Fallview Tavern & Grille at the top of the waterfalls. I released my grip on him, and he helped me off the motorcycle.

"It's turning out to be a nice evening. I thought we'd eat on the patio. Is that okay with you?" Kai motioned for me to lead the way to the doors.

"Yeah, that's fine." I looked around, once again taking in the majestic view of the mountainside. Once we entered the establishment, the ambiance was quite different. I always thought of a dungeon when I stepped through those doors. It was kind of cool, and I supposed the dimmer lighting was romantic for real couples. But I wasn't interested in being in a dark corner with Kai. As he'd suggested, the seating outside suited us much better.

We were shown to a table on the patio and given menus. I scanned the list of great food, but once again those butterflies were pushing out any thoughts of eating, despite the fact that I'd been starving earlier. It made no sense to me. I had nothing to be nervous about, unless you counted the fact that we lied to a hellhound. And that if we didn't pull this entire scheme off, not only would we be in hot water with the club, but I may lose my only chance at learning more about my father or why I'd been feeling so weird. No, nothing to be anxious about at all.

"What sounds good?" Kai asked as he looked over his menu.

"Honestly, I don't know. Do you even eat human food? I've seen you pick at stuff at school, but I don't think I've ever seen you really eat a full meal."

He flipped to the back of the menu. "Sometimes. It's not horrible, most of the time. Don't expect me to eat kale, though. That's never gonna happen."

I laughed. "Yeah, me neither. Who looked at grass and thought 'Yeah, let's eat that?'"

He smiled. "Someone who hadn't yet discovered steak."

I nodded, still laughing. "Preferably rare steak."

Kai put down his menu and leaned forward. "Oh yeah. Now that's good. All that blood . . ."

We both stared at each other for a moment.

He broke the silence first. "Honestly, that's the only thing that sounds good right now."

"Steak?" I asked.

"No, blood." He looked around, assuring no one was sitting close enough to overhear our conversation.

"Yeah, it does," I agreed, except we were on different pages with that. Like most other vampires, he drank human blood. I drank animal blood. Many thought it was an ethical thing for me, and I allowed that to be my publicly known reasoning, but in truth it was a little more complicated than that. Human blood made me ill, and I didn't know why, but I couldn't keep it down.

"Would you . . ." He paused and seemed to be searching for the right words. "Do you want to go . . . get some?"

"I don't think that would work well, Kai. I only drink animal blood. Besides, isn't the whole point of this exercise to be seen together in public?"

He nodded. "We've been seen here and on the bike. And there are things we can do later as well. We don't have to do all our convincing in one night. That wouldn't work anyway."

"My supply is at home and—"

Kai cut me off. "Let's hunt for it." His voice held a tinge of excitement.

"What?" I'd never hunted. Ever.

"Get it fresh. It's amazing that way." When I frowned, he groaned. "C'mon, Miranda. Live a little. It's easy. I can teach you."

For some reason, his earlier assertion that I didn't know how to enjoy myself had poked a sore spot. And now he'd poked it again. "What about you? I'm not going to watch you hunt humans."

He shook his head. "You won't have to. I'll hunt animals, too."

"Really, you don't have to do that just for me."

"I'm not doing it for you. I drink animal blood, too. I switched to it about a year ago." Ugh. He smirked.

I had to look like a fish out of water, with my mouth gaping open like a trout. I wasn't sure what I was hearing. Kai and his buddies were the kind of vampires that mocked others for not drinking what they called "real" blood.

"Excuse me? I must have something in my ears. I thought I heard you say you drink animal blood."

He nodded. "I do. Almost exclusively."

"Why?" I managed to stammer.

"You don't have the market cornered on ethics, you know. Others can decide to be more humanitarian." He crossed his arms.

I wondered if I'd actually offended him. "I didn't say I did. I was just surprised. What do your parents say about that?"

He frowned. "I'd rather not bring them into this. I've been having a good time so far and would like to keep it that way."

"Okay then." I was once again at a loss for words. Why all the hostility toward his parents? I thought they were a close family.

"So, are we gonna hunt or not?" There was that excitement again.

"Well, I guess. I don't think I'm properly dressed for it, though."

He smiled and stood, reaching his hand for mine. I placed my palm in his, and he pulled me to my feet. Nikki, our waitress, walked up to us at that moment.

"Sorry, we've had a sudden change of plans." Kai released my hand and pulled out his wallet. He dug out a twenty dollar bill and gave it to her. "That's the tip I would have given you if we'd stayed."

She smiled. "Thanks!"

He took my hand in his once more and pulled me through the building and back out the front doors. We reached the bike and were seated in moments. He drove us farther up the mountain, and all the while, I wondered what I had just gotten myself into.

CHAPTER 6

We were moving farther up the mountain and once again picking up speed. I closed my eyes this time. I couldn't believe what I was about to do, and who I was about to do it with. Hunting animals with Kai Reynolds. Nothing about that seemed sane.

He eventually pulled off onto a small dirt road, and once we'd traveled the dusty path several feet back into the trees, he parked.

After we'd both dismounted, he turned to face me. "So here's the thing about hunting. You have to be calm and steady. It takes a few tries to catch something your first time out."

"How many times have you done this?" I was surprised he knew how to do any of this. And how did he expect to catch them? We easily moved faster than humans, but I'd never raced a wolf or a bear. Could we outrun those? A terrible thought occurred to me, and I gripped his arm. "Kai, how will we know if an animal is just an animal and not a shifter?"

He squeezed my hand. "Don't worry, you'll know. Shifters give off a different smell. There is a slight tinge of human. Just enough that you can tell the difference. The tattoos help us identify each other as well." He pointed to the magic infused tattoo he had to get when registering as a supernatural being in Havenwood Falls. We all had one. It was necessary to keep track of everyone and assure the rules from the Court were being upheld.

"Oh, yeah. That's good." I was relieved to hear that. I'd never forgive myself if we attacked a local.

"Just follow my lead. I think you'll find certain parts of it come naturally." He quietly stepped into the tree line, and I followed.

I highly doubted any of this would be second nature, but I'd do my best.

The forest floor was already showing the telltale signs of fall. Colorful leaves scattered here and there, still mostly damp from the abundance of rain we'd had in August. Twigs and branches intermingled with weeds and wildflowers. Crickets chirped as the sun began to set. Squirrels scampered up the trunks as we passed by. The beauty of nature was serene, even as the darkness descended on us. It seemed a shame that we were about to disrupt that calm with our activities.

I focused on walking as quietly as I could, tracing Kai's steps exactly. Thank the stars for vampire night vision. We'd traveled a good distance from the original trail when he put his hand up to stop me. I froze, listening for any sign of . . . something. I wasn't sure what I was supposed to be doing. He put his finger to his lips, then motioned for me to stand beside him.

I did as instructed, allowing my eyes to roam the vast forest around us. All I could see were trees. We were engulfed by them.

He pulled me in front of him and pressed his chest against my back. With his lips at my ear, he whispered instructions to me.

"Do you hear that?"

I shook my head.

"Just take some calming breaths and listen."

I took several deep breaths, allowing my body to relax and my mind to clear. That's when I heard it. The sound of something walking in our direction. It had a light step, but I was sure it had four legs.

"Do you hear it now?" he whispered again.

I nodded, afraid that if I spoke, I'd scare whatever it was away.

"Keep your mind clear. The closer it gets, the more you can hear."

I focused on the sounds I was hearing, trying to drown out any other senses, which was complicated with Kai touching me so much. The closer it came, the more I heard. In moments I could hear minute things—like the breath from its nostrils and the pounding of its heart. I felt my own adrenaline kick up a notch in response.

Kai must have sensed my reaction, or more likely he knew what I was feeling because he felt it too. "Do you feel that excitement? That's our instinct. We know prey is near."

I wanted to ask why I'd never felt that before. I'd been around animals plenty of times and never wanted to attack them. Why was this different? But I'd have to save that for later. Right now I could only focus on the task at hand.

"Now start adding your sense of smell to your tools. Are you picking up on that musk?"

"Yes," I whispered. "What is it?"

"A buck."

I felt my eyes go wide, and I turned my face to his. "We're gonna take down a buck?"

He smiled. "Yes, ma'am."

I wasn't sure I was ready for this, even with all the adrenaline spurring me on.

"We'll tag team this one, since it's your first time. When he gets close, I'll grab the rack and take him to the ground. You go for the jugular."

"I've never done that before!" I could hear the panic in my own voice, despite being able to keep it at a whisper.

"More instinct. You'll know what to do when the time is right."

I groaned. "You'd better be right, Kai."

He patted me on the shoulder. "I'm never wrong."

"That's a debate for later," I murmured.

We both stood very still as the buck neared the tree we were standing behind. In an instant, Kai had jumped out and grabbed the large deer's rack. He was so fast that the buck didn't have time to register what was happening before he tried to escape.

Kai's vampire strength kicked in, and he wrenched the animal's large head to the left, causing its body to twist in response. The buck went down hard, and as Kai had said it would, my instinct kicked in. I lunged, landing on top of the beast. I felt my fangs extend from my gums, and the only thing I could hear was the blood running through the buck's veins. It called to me. I could almost taste it. And without having to think about it, I sank my teeth into its neck.

It was euphoric.

It was satisfying.

It was delicious.

And for a few moments, I was immersed in the feeding.

But then the more human side of my brain began to slowly filter back in. What I had just done ran like an instant replay in my mind. A sob escaped my throat, and my heart sank as I pulled back. Without even thinking, I ran my hands over my face and then down my pants. Blood dripped from my chin onto my clothing. Blood also ran from the wounds on the buck's neck.

Kai growled. "You're wasting it!"

Then he jumped to the other side of the buck and fed from the spot I had just vacated.

I fell back on my butt, my hands behind me and supporting my upper body. I watched in terror and fascination as Kai finished draining the life of the animal we'd just hunted. I saw the buck's breathing slow and then stop. I heard the heart beat for the last time.

A tear ran down my cheek, cutting a trail through the blood that still covered the lower half of my face.

Kai looked up, a satisfied smile on his face, until he saw me. "Are you okay?" He moved closer and crouched in front of me. "What's wrong?"

I couldn't speak. The tears just kept flowing.

"Miranda, I didn't mean to yell at you for wasting the blood. I know this is all new to you." The look he gave me was genuinely apologetic.

I shook my head. "It's not you." I took a deep breath, trying not to let a sob escape. "I've just never taken a life before. I didn't expect it to be this hard."

He nodded. "Yeah, that takes some adjusting to. But look at it this way—if we didn't, some hunter would have come along and got him. Or a mountain lion. This way we feed, and then leave the carcass here for the carnivores to feed on as well."

"Yeah, I guess." I wiped another tear away.

"Miranda, it's the cycle of life. For something to live, something else has to die. Plants die and feed the buck. The buck dies and feeds the carnivore. The carnivore dies and feeds the soil. The soil feeds the plant. Full circle." He gave me a small smile.

"Except in this case, the carnivore doesn't die. We've cheated nature."

"Well, true. But who knows what's ahead? I'm sure it all balances out somehow." He stood and offered me his hand.

I took it, and he helped me up. "So we just leave it here?"

"Yeah, it won't take long for the other animals to find it. I imagine by now they are already closing in. The smell of blood draws them in quickly. They'll come out of hiding once the more dangerous predators leave."

"More dangerous predators?" I asked.

"Us." He smiled.

We started to walk back the direction we came. I focused on the logic in his explanation to help control my emotions.

"So," he said, "aside from the sad part, did you enjoy hunting?"

I nodded, surprised at my answer. "I really did. There was something exhilarating about it. And it tasted . . ."

"Better than the bagged and bottled stuff, right?"

I chuckled. "Yes, much better."

"I knew you'd love it." He turned and started walking backwards so he could face me while we walked. "Although, we're gonna have to get you a huge bib if you continue to be so messy."

I glanced down at myself. It looked like I'd barely escaped a horror flick. "Oh, crap. This was my favorite shirt, too."

"Well, I'm gonna say that's a goner. You might as well use the rest of it to clean off your face."

I stopped and turned my back to him, using the bottom of my

shirt to wipe my cheeks, mouth, and chin. I faced him again. "Did I get it?"

"Meh, enough. You still look like a psycho Barbie doll." He turned back around and started to jog away.

"Hey! You aren't insulting me and then leaving me behind, mister!" I hurried to catch up.

CHAPTER 7

*W*e'd only been back in town a few minutes when Kai tapped my leg.

I leaned forward.

"We're being followed."

I looked back to see a dark-clothed man on a motorcycle a few car lengths behind us.

I again leaned forward as much as I could and tried to speak to Kai without having to scream over the engine. "Who is that guy?"

"I'll introduce you when we stop. Just follow my lead, to the letter. Got it?"

I nodded. "Got it."

I looked down and remembered I was a quite a mess. Blood stained my white top in several places, and there were random splatters and streaks on my jeans. *Kai's right. I'll have to trash the shirt. There's no getting that mess out.* I then remembered that SIN members weren't likely strangers to blood. It wouldn't faze them a bit.

We pulled in front of the club, and the other biker pulled up next to us. Kai shut off the engine and turned to face the man.

"Hey, Monte, what's up?" Kai kept his face impassive, but I could feel the tension in him as he helped me off his motorcycle.

Monte wasn't an imposing figure, with his tall, slight frame and scruffy features, but I caught myself wanting to hold Kai's hand for reassurance.

"Just takin' care of some business." He gave Kai a pointed look.

"Cool. Miranda and I were just up in the mountains doing a little hunting." He gestured to my blood-soaked shirt. "She's a little new to it, so she's still getting the hang of a clean feed."

Monte looked me up and down, and this time I did move closer to Kai and grasped his hand. He squeezed mine in return.

He chuckled. "She's a messy eater."

I fought back the urge to say something rude. Instead I held my tongue.

Kai put his arm around me and squeezed. "We'll fix that, right, babe?"

I looked up into his face and did my best to paste on a sweet smile. I could feel my teeth grinding together. "With your help, I'll be a pro in no time, stud."

Kai's eyebrows drew together in warning. "You know I love it when you talk dirty."

I continued to smile at him, hoping Monte would buy our horrible acting so we could go.

He turned and took a few steps toward the front door, then stopped and looked back at us. "Well? You coming or not?"

Kai nodded. "Sure, I just need a moment alone with my girl, if you don't mind."

"Sure." He opened the door and stepped inside the club just as Kai pulled me close.

There was a moment when I was sure Kai was actually going to kiss me. I was totally unprepared for it. And then I found I was even more unprepared for what happened next.

He put his forehead against mine. "Okay, we are expected to go inside. I'm supposed to introduce you to the guys. Be cool, pretend you're having fun. I'll take care of the rest. And don't cringe at anything you hear or see. They get kind of . . ."

"Debased?" I finished for him.

"Something like that," he muttered, then released a deep sigh. "I'll get you out of there as quick as I can."

I stepped back, putting some distance between us. "You forget, I've seen the inside before."

"That's when the lights were down and you only got a quick glimpse. This will be different."

I was starting to rethink this whole plan of his. Surely I could find information about my dad some other way. Did I really need Kai or the club's help? The reality of it was that I absolutely did. They were my best shot at getting answers.

I straightened my spine. "Okay then, lead the way."

Kai put his arm around me, and we walked through the door together.

We entered the busy clubhouse. There was a big guy sitting at the bar quickly downing a beer. He appeared to be all muscle and had long, dirty-blond hair with a beard that matched. He turned to face us.

Kai moved his arm from my shoulders to my waist in a more intimate, possessive gesture. "Hey, Crusher, this is my girl, Miranda."

Crusher smiled, lifted the bottle a bit and gave a small acknowledgment with two fingers, then swiveled his seat back to facing the bar.

Kai lowered his lips to my ear. "Let's hope they all go that easy."

"Yeah," I whispered. Having him that close was disorienting.

He guided me toward the middle of the room and surprised me with an announcement. "Hey, everyone! This is my girl, Miranda."

Several beers rose in greeting, and a couple of the women sitting on the laps of two of the men smiled and nodded, although I wasn't sure how genuine those smiles were. I was already uncomfortable, and we'd been inside less than five minutes.

Kai pulled out a wooden chair, which looked to be the cleanest spot in the room, and motioned for me to take a seat. "I'll pick some music."

He walked to the jukebox and stood next to Monte. They chatted quietly while I assumed they looked through music. Kai finally picked a song, and some Five Finger Death Punch poured out of the speakers.

Kai sat next to me on a sofa that looked pretty nasty. Monte sat next to him and looked me over.

"You seem like a nice girl. Why you datin' a jerk like Kai?"

Kai flipped Monte the bird. "I'm not all bad."

Monte snorted. "You sure ain't all good."

"Stop busting my chops, dude. You're making me look bad in front of her." Kai turned his attention to me. "Don't listen to him. He's just jealous that I have such a gorgeous girl all to myself."

I knew it was all part of the act, but dang it all . . . I actually blushed. I felt the heat rise to my cheeks. I didn't even know vampires could blush, but there it was. Kai noticed it, too. He looked at me and for a split second seemed to lose his train of thought. Thankfully, he recovered quickly.

"I'll admit, she's too good for me. And it's getting late. If I don't get her home soon, her mother may never let me take her out again."

A loud snicker came from Crusher at the bar. I had a feeling Kai was gonna catch a lot of crap over this visit later.

"I'll bring her back when we can stay longer." Kai nodded at Monte.

Monte shot him another look that I couldn't decipher, then took a swig of the beer in his hand. "Yeah, I don't think her momma would be too thrilled to learn she's hangin' out with us."

My eyes shot to his. "You know my mom?"

"Not really, but any self-respecting parent would have a coronary if they learned their little girl was seen in this club."

I wanted to remind him that I'm not all that little, and in a year or so would be making my own decisions, no matter what anyone else said. Kai didn't give me that opportunity.

"I'd appreciate it if you kept her visit here just among the group. It'll be bad enough when people realize I'm part of SIN."

Monte slapped Kai on the back. "You can count on us, bruh." He turned his eyes to me. "Have a good night, Miss Miranda." Then he found a seat at the bar and left us to show ourselves out.

We made it to the motorcycle, and I put my hands on my hips. "What just happened in there?"

He raised one eyebrow. "What do you mean? We got lucky. We didn't have to spend much time with the crew tonight."

"No, I mean all the 'she's too good for me' stuff. How does that help them believe we're an item if we don't seem like a good match?" It didn't make sense to me.

"That's just it. We aren't a good match. Everyone knows you're Miss Goody Two-Shoes." He jerked his head in the direction of the club. "Even those guys. So I have to make it look like I'm winning you over slowly. Getting your mom's approval. Wearing your perfect persona down a bit, so that we'd eventually make a better pair."

"That just sounds . . . weird. And I am not Miss Goody Two-Shoes!" I wasn't a troublemaker, but still, I wasn't perfect or even pretending to be. I couldn't help if that's how people perceived me.

"Uh huh. You just keep telling yourself that." And there was the smirk. I wondered if he'd think I was so innocent if he knew how much I wanted to rip his lips off in that moment.

"Take me home." I was tired and ready to get out of my bloody clothes. And I still had to come up with an excuse for my appearance. Mom would not have approved of my hunting.

Kai drove to my house slowly, which surprised me. I assumed he was as ready to end this false date as I was. But instead of his normal kamikaze speed, it was actually a pleasant, almost relaxing ride.

We pulled into the driveway, and I quickly hopped off the motorcycle.

"Wait." Kai was right behind me. "You can't just run in."

I turned to face him. "And why is that? The night's over, right?"

"Yes, but this isn't usually how a date ends." He hitched his thumbs in his belt loops.

"You expect a kiss?" I didn't think I could've been more surprised if my teeth had sprouted wings and flew out of my mouth.

"Not a real one. It just has to look like it."

"You think they have spies in my neighborhood? You are really paranoid, you know that?" I was starting to wonder about his sanity.

He stepped forward, closing the gap between us. "Miranda, we can't be too careful. I don't know who may or may not be keeping tabs on us. You don't have to be a member of SIN to be reporting in. They can afford to pay average people to share information."

I looked up at him. "Do you really believe that?"

"I'm afraid not to. We can't take any risks."

"How long do we have to play this game?" I didn't know how long I could keep up the ruse.

"Until we find the information you need. Or, if you decide you don't want to know more, we can end it early, once we are sure we've convinced them it wasn't a lie to begin with. We can stage a big fight or something." He shrugged. "I'm sorry it's come to this."

"It's not your fault. I'm the one that got caught sneaking into the club." I sighed.

"Oh yeah, it is all your fault."

I smacked his arm. "Don't push your luck."

He laughed.

"Okay, so what do we do to fake a kiss?" My palms were a little sweaty just thinking about it.

"Well, I guess we just put our faces close to each other so it looks like our lips are touching."

"You guess?" For someone with all the plans, he sure was uncertain about some parts.

"Well, excuse me. I've never had to fake a kiss before. Up to this point, all my dates have actually wanted to kiss me." His tone gave away his annoyance. Could his ego have been hurt a smidgen? I couldn't muster an ounce of sympathy for him.

"Well, mark this down as date number one that definitely does not want to kiss you. At all."

His jaw clenched a little. I was getting to him. I shouldn't have enjoyed it so much, but this was a side of him I'd rarely seen. I couldn't let it go just yet.

"In fact, I can probably think of several other people I'd rather be kissing right now instead of you."

That must have been too far.

He put his face close to mine. "Well, let's get this horrible experience over with then, shall we?"

I nodded.

He pulled me against him and pressed his lips to mine. I was caught completely off guard. I grabbed ahold of him to keep from falling backward, and at the same time, his hands slid around my lower back and pressed me close. I wasn't sure how to respond. The pressure of his lips started out almost punishing, but quickly changed to something more gentle. It didn't take me long to realize that there was nothing fake about this kiss.

I couldn't decide whether to push him away or melt into the warmth of his arms. Seemingly against my own better judgment, I'd given in to the kiss, allowing my lips to relax under his. My senses were a little hazy when Kai finally pulled away.

He looked down at me and smiled. "I hope that wasn't too disgusting for you."

It took me longer than I would have liked to register that his intent was to prove me wrong. I felt the anger build, and I balled my hands into fists.

"Why you . . ." I started to stammer, unable to find the right words to express my feelings.

He placed a finger on my lips. "Don't say or do anything you'll regret later." He turned and got on his motorcycle. As he started the engine, I finally found my voice.

"I already have," I growled. Then I turned on my heel and disappeared inside.

Once the door shut behind me, I leaned against it and took a deep breath. *What was that? Why did I enjoy that? Why am I admitting I enjoyed that?* I was sure I was losing my mind. Kai was not my type and never would be. My mind flashed back to my conversation with Jetta at Coffee Haven. She'd said she sensed sparks between us, but even if that were true, it didn't mean we were good for each other.

Mom walked into the living room. "Miranda, you're home. How was your date?"

I shrugged. "It was okay." I didn't want to talk about it.

She looked down at my clothes. "What happened? Are you okay?" The alarm caused her voice to raise an octave.

I looked down at my shirt. "It's not my blood."

She crossed her arms. "Then whose is it?"

"No one's." I wasn't sure how to explain this.

"Miranda, it has to belong to someone. Blood doesn't come out of trees."

I rubbed my hand over my face. "Well, it belongs to something, not someone."

I'd heard it said that the truth will set you free. I was about to put that to the test.

She motioned to the sofa. "Sit. Explain."

I moved next to her and sunk into the cushions, exhaustion from the day starting to catch up with me. "Kai and I were at the restaurant, and nothing sounded good, so we went on an impromptu hunt up the mountain."

Her eyes went wide. "You hunted? Animals? With Kai?"

I nodded but didn't answer otherwise.

She looked at my clothes once more, then back at my face. "Did you actually get any in your mouth?"

"Mom!" I snapped.

She started to giggle. "It looks like you hit a major artery, and then it shot around like a runaway fire hose." She started to wheeze between even deeper laughs.

I was shocked she wasn't chastising me, but also relieved. And she was laughing. Something I didn't witness nearly enough. I started to laugh, too. "It does look pretty bad, doesn't it? But I did get full, so it wasn't a total loss."

She put her arms around me and pulled me in for a hug. "Well, that had to be a new experience. I'm not really sure how I feel about it. What did you think?"

"I'm not sure myself. Parts of it were exhilarating. Other parts were very sad. You're not mad?"

She shook her head. "No, I'm not mad. That's how I figured you'd feel. I hadn't suggested you go before because I wasn't sure you were emotionally ready for a kill. You love animals so much . . . and taking a life isn't easy, especially the first time."

"Did you ever hunt?" I felt the sting of tears prick my eyes, the vision of the deer taking its last breath as Kai drained the life from it still vivid in my mind.

She cleared her throat. "Yes, a few times."

"How did you handle it?"

She pressed her lips together. "It's not a time I'm very proud of, sweetheart. I wasn't the person I am now."

Baxter. She was talking about when she was with my father. Another thought pushed through my mind. She didn't take to animal blood the way I did. She drank human blood. She'd probably hunted humans. I suddenly felt a little ill.

"I'm pretty tired. I think I'll get to bed." I stood.

"But aren't you going to tell me about Kai? I didn't even know you were interested in him."

"Neither did I, Mom." And that was a truth I wasn't sure how to deal with. "I'll talk to you about it in the morning, once I've had some sleep, okay?" *And I've had time to make up a backstory.*

"All right. Good night, sweetheart." She kissed my forehead.

"Good night, Mom." I quickly made my way down the hall to my bedroom, the need to be alone driving me forward. Tonight was quite possibly the craziest experience of my life. I'd hunted, helped kill, and fed on my first live prey; sat in the den of the most dangerous men in town and survived; learned my mom used to hunt humans; and scariest of all, I discovered that I'm physically attracted to Kai Reynolds. This was not good. Not good at all.

CHAPTER 8

*T*he next day was Labor Day, so we had the day off from school. I hadn't made any plans and spent most of my time catching up on some chores for Mom around the house. Since she'd been sick, she hadn't been able to keep up with her part of the cleaning list as easily.

Mom had planned on working, but woke up that morning feeling pretty bad. She was actually throwing up—something I'd never seen before. She couldn't keep blood or food down. When I wasn't cleaning, I stayed by her bedside, helping her in any way I could. She didn't need me often, but I didn't feel comfortable leaving her alone. At my insistence, she'd given me the number of Dr. Underwood so I could reach him in case of an emergency. She was sure a day of rest was really all she required. I worried she was in need of so much more.

The entire day had gone by before I heard from Kai again. I was starting to wonder if the kiss we'd shared had repulsed him so much that he didn't even want to look at or talk to me. I hadn't gone on many dates, to be perfectly honest. I'd always been very careful. Some guys were nice enough, but didn't hold my interest. Others had reputations that kept me as far away from them as possible. So far I hadn't found anyone that interested me both intellectually and physically. Kai ticked that last box, as I'd realized the previous evening, and I knew he was a smart guy. That didn't mean we meshed on a psychological level, but he did have both attributes in his favor. When it came down to it, how I felt about Kai didn't matter. We were acting a part to get information, then we would go our separate ways.

The doorbell rang around nine-thirty p.m. I'd just finished giving Mom some water and putting a cool cloth on her head.

When I opened the door, Kai was standing there.

"Hi." He looked tired.

"Hello." I looked like a wreck. My hair was falling out of the bun I'd put it in earlier in the day, and I was wearing an old T-shirt and sweatpants. Seeing Kai brought out a self-conscious side I didn't know I had. I caught myself trying to shove my hair back into place.

"Can I come in?" He gave me a nervous smile.

"Oh, yeah. Sure." I stepped aside and allowed him to walk past me, then closed the door behind him.

"I may have some news for you."

"Okay." I was ready for anything that might move our plan forward and get it over with quicker. I motioned for him to sit at the kitchen table while I rushed to Mom's room to make sure she was asleep. I shut her bedroom door, hoping to muffle our conversation even more.

Kai cleared his throat as I took a seat. "I was sitting in the conference room, sorting some stuff for Liam, when I overheard him ask Monte about our visit yesterday. Of course I was on high alert then, trying to catch every word I could. Liam didn't seem to mind that I'd brought you with me. He was more interested in your mom."

That caught my attention. "Why would he be interested in her?"

"I didn't get that part. But I did hear him say that he felt bad about all Baxter had put her through . . . and was still putting her through."

"That doesn't make sense. He's not been in her life since before I was born." It felt like I was ending up with more questions than answers.

"He also kept mentioning someone he called Doc, but it didn't sound like Liam liked him very much. There were other names he called the man that were not things you'd say in polite company."

I shifted in my chair. "This just gets weirder and weirder."

Kai nodded. "I don't understand the connection either, but it's a start."

"Yeah, I guess."

We sat in an awkward silence for a few moments. I tried to think of something to say that wouldn't bring up last night.

"My mom's been sick today."

"Sick? How is she sick?" His voice held the same confusion mine did when I first received the news.

"I don't know. We're trying to figure it out. I'm sure you've heard the stories . . . about my mom and me." I glanced at him quickly, then looked away. "How we aren't like other vampires."

"I'm sorry to hear she's not well." He didn't acknowledge the stories surrounding my birth. He just leaned back, acting as if I'd never brought them up. And while I wasn't looking directly at him, I could feel his eyes on me.

"I should go check on her." I stood, trying to appear calm despite the butterflies in my stomach.

"Please tell her I hope she's feeling better soon." He stood as well. "Before I go, I wanted to talk to you about something."

I groaned inwardly. I did not want to have this discussion right now. Maybe ever.

"I wanted to apologize for last night. I honestly didn't intend to kiss you like that, but you'd been insulting me and . . . I guess my bruised ego took over."

I shook my head. "I owe you the apology. I was being rude."

He smiled. "So we're even then? Your rude cancels my ego trip?"

I couldn't help but return his grin. "I guess that works."

"Great. Go check on your mom, then call me in the morning. I'll let you know what else I've found."

"I have school in the morning, so it may be after three before I can call. You're going back to look for more info?" I was starting to think we should quit while we were ahead.

"Sure. To be honest, I'm pretty curious now. And lately there hasn't been a whole lot for me to do around the club, besides clean up after the parties. It allows me to snoop a little."

I frowned. "I don't know, Kai. Mom is sick, and SIN is watching our every move. Maybe it's best if we just call the whole thing off."

He crossed his arms in front of his chest. "Are you chickening out on me? After all I've gone through? I never took you for a quitter."

"I'm not a quitter. I'm just concerned." I glanced back at my mother's bedroom. "She's really sick. I've never seen her this way. I'm scared. Dr. Underwood hasn't found any answers yet."

He pulled me in for a hug, and I didn't push away. I needed the comfort he was offering in that moment. "I'm sure it'll be okay. Someone will figure out what's going on."

AROUND MIDNIGHT I checked on Mom one last time before I went to bed. Her fever had broken, and she seemed to be sleeping better. Kai had left around ten p.m., and my mind had been racing ever since. I tossed and turned for a good hour before I decided to get up and read. I went to the small bookshelf in my room and ran my fingers over the spines, searching for a book that would take me away from the mess my mind was in. It would suck tomorrow when I was exhausted at school, but better to keep my mind occupied than lay there and worry about the worst possible scenario.

I settled in on the window seat across from my bed with a well-worn copy of *Sense and Sensibility* when a loud knock on the glass next to my head almost made me scream. My reaction was to toss the book and fall off the seat, landing hard on the floor.

My heart raced as I looked up to see Kai tapping on my window. My fear turned to annoyance.

I got up and turned the latch, then pushed the window up. "What in the world do you think you're doing?" I whispered in anger.

"My parents kicked me out." He tossed a duffel bag past me, and it landed on the floor with a loud thud.

"Why?" I couldn't take my eyes off the bag sitting in the middle of my bedroom floor.

"They don't like some of the things I'm doing." He climbed through the window and sat on the floor. I joined him on the floor, facing him.

"Like what?" I couldn't imagine him committing any offense that would push his parents that far.

"They found out I'm part of SIN."

"Oh." That did make sense.

"Oddly enough, that wasn't what they threw the biggest fit over." He leaned back against the foot of my bed and rested his forearms on his knees.

"What's worse than joining a notorious biker gang that may or may not be involved in unspeakable acts?"

He raised his eyes to mine. "Apparently, dating you."

I swallowed hard. "Me?" I felt my heart break a little. Not that I'd expected his parents to like me. We weren't even really dating. But to know that anyone thought so little of me, especially when I'd worked so hard to develop a respectable reputation—it hurt. "What's so wrong with me?"

He sat forward and put his hands on top of mine. "Absolutely nothing. Nothing is wrong with you. It's them. They're . . . terrible people." He sighed. "During our fight, I learned a little more about your mom and dad."

"That's good." I pushed down my self-consciousness so I could concentrate on this new information.

"Well, it is and it isn't. I think we have to see this thing through. Your mom's life may depend on it." He gave my hands a squeeze.

I took a moment to soak that in. "Continue."

"Mom said I'd regret being with someone like you. When I asked her to clarify, she said that you're not a true vampire and that we'd never be happy together. That your dad ruined your mom's vampiric purity. Dad jumped in and told her to shut up. He said that no one was supposed to talk about that, and it was just gossip anyway. So I pushed further." He dropped my hands. "Mom pulled me aside as I was packing my bag. She told me that I really needed to understand what I was getting into. To ask the club about Doc and his experiments. That's all she'd say."

"So maybe whatever is making my mom sick has something to do with this Doc guy?" I was worried and hopeful at the same time.

He nodded. "That's how I took it. Maybe he's the one we need to find. He might know how to help her, since no one else around here seems to have a clue yet."

"If that's the case, then we definitely can't give up." I couldn't walk away if it would help my mom, no matter how uncertain I felt.

"I'll see what I can learn about Doc. Maybe Liam or Savage will be willing to talk to me about it." He ran a hand through his hair, messing it up slightly.

The thought of him approaching the very people we were warned to avoid made me nervous for Kai, but I didn't know if we had any other options. "Okay, just be careful. The more we dig into this, the worse I feel about the whole situation."

"It'll be fine, Miranda. We'll figure it all out and find help for your mom. Maybe we'll even learn about your dad as well, just like we'd intended."

"I hope you're right." But I had my reservations.

He picked up his bag and tossed it back out the window. "I'm staying at the clubhouse for now. Not sure if I'll try to get my own place yet. I'll have to get a job first. No more freeloading. Gotta stop living the good life off Mom and Pops's money." He grinned, and I got the feeling he didn't mind that one bit.

He moved to climb out the window, but I stopped him. "Kai, can I ask you something personal?"

He turned and sat down on the padded seat. "Sure. Can't promise I'll answer."

I smiled a little. "I know they aren't your real parents. I mean . . . you weren't born into this, like I was. You were turned, right?"

He nodded. "Yeah."

"So, when were you turned?" It had just dawned on me that his family wasn't actually family.

"Shortly after my seventeenth birthday." He looked down at his hands, and I worried that my questions made him uncomfortable.

"If you don't want to answer . . ."

"No, it's fine. It's just . . . weird." He looked up at me. "Susanna and Zeke were turned in the early 1900s. They traveled a lot, always looking for the next best thing to elevate their status among other vampires. Money, power, status—that's all they care about. Then one day they found me. I'd run away from an abusive father, quit school, and was living on the streets. I guess they decided they needed a son to complete the perfect family picture. So they turned me and trained me to be the ideal mini Reynolds."

"How long have you been with them?"

He thought about it a minute. "Well, let's see. I moved here two and a half years ago, so . . . just a little over that."

"So you would have been nineteen, had you lived?"

"Yeah, but I'm technically seventeen forever now." He smiled. "On my last birthday I baked myself a huge cake and invited them into the dining room for a toast."

"That was nice," I said.

He chuckled. "No, it wasn't. No one knows this about me, but I appreciate a good prank. I knew they weren't going to touch the cake, since they don't approve of human food anymore, so I explained that it was a symbolic celebration of my new birth and life with them. They seemed to fall for that, so once we were all in the room, I lit the candles." He put his hand over his eyes, and his shoulders were shaking. "They weren't really candles. They were firecrackers, which were connected to even more firecrackers inside the cake." He laughed openly now. "There was cake and icing everywhere. They were so pissed."

I laughed, too, as I envisioned his stuffy parents with icing and cake all over them.

"But what were they gonna do? They made me immortal. It wasn't like they were gonna kill me. Then who'd they get to be their errand boy and do the dirty work for them? I'm just so sick of it all."

"What do you mean?" I knew I was prying, but I wanted to

understand this side of Kai's life.

He shrugged. "I'm tired of pretending to be like them. The night of the Cold Moon Ball, I told them I thought Mr. Mills's plan was a horrible thing to do to Zoey. I didn't want any part of it. We argued for almost an hour, until Zeke physically hauled me to the Annex." He shook his head. "It's always like that. I'm expected to do everything they, or anyone in their circle, asks of me. Even if it's despicable. When you have that many people pushing you, it's hard to say no." He laughed. "It's funny—as much as I hate them, they did me a favor. I was hungry, dirty, and sick when they found me in that alley. They promised me a good life, and they've given it to me. I just didn't understand the costs at the time. But I'm making the best of it. And it'll be even better now that I'm out from under their thumb."

"Are you really out?" The break seemed too easy. Too clean.

"They'll demand I come back. They always do this when I step out of line. They kick me out, then they decide their reputations as fabulous parents with the perfect, conveniently obedient son are more important and try to lure me back in. I'm not going back this time."

"Well, if you need anything, I'm here to help. It's the least I can do after all you've done for me."

He climbed out the window then leaned the upper half of his torso in through the opening. "There is one thing you can do."

"Sure, what is it?"

He crooked his index finger in a come-hither motion. I stood and moved close to the window.

"I need to know something." His voice was barely a whisper, so I leaned closer.

He looked down, and I couldn't see his eyes.

"Kai?"

When he raised his face to mine, he was wearing that smirk that I hated. Correction—used to hate. It was starting to grow on me. "Did you really hate my kiss last night?"

I felt the heat rush to my cheeks once again. "Umm . . . I . . ."

"Glad to hear it." Then he backed away and was gone.

Nope. I take that back. I still hated that smirk.

CHAPTER 9

School the next day was excruciating. I tried to concentrate on my first two classes, but I couldn't get Kai's conversation with his parents out of my mind. Waiting until school was over was going to kill me.

The bell rang, and I put my books in my locker, grabbing what I needed for third period. I'd just passed one of the janitorial closets when a hand wrapped around my mouth and pulled me inside. The door slammed behind me. I lashed out, trying to hit whoever it was that had grabbed me.

"Stop it, Miranda. It's me," Kai hissed. He removed his hand from my mouth and stepped back.

The closet was dark, so I searched for the light switch. Once I flipped it on, I glared at him. "You gotta stop grabbing me like that! You couldn't say 'Hello' like a normal person?"

"I'm not a normal person. And no, not for what we're about to do."

I raised my eyebrows. "What are we about to do?"

"You're ditching school for the rest of the day." He beamed as if he'd just learned he'd won a prize.

I shook my head. "No, you're nuts. That's not a good idea."

"It's perfect! You do something out of character, which shows SIN I'm rubbing off on you, and we get a chance to do some research on Doc." He pulled a sheet of paper out of his pocket.

"You found something?"

"Sort of." He wiggled it in front of my face. "But we can't discuss it here. Are you coming with me or not?"

I sighed. "I . . ."

I wasn't sure what to do. Skipping school might go on my record. And what would my mother say?

"C'mon, Miranda. Take a chance. Live a little before you die, in a manner of speaking." He winked at me.

I groaned.

"You know you want to." He poked me in the ribs, which was a ticklish spot for me.

I jumped. "Stop."

"You want to go, and you can't say no to me." He poked me again.

"Kai . . ." I warned as I jumped away again.

"Stop playing hard to get."

I froze. I wasn't sure how he meant that. "I'm not."

He crossed his eyes and tucked his upper lip under where I could see his teeth and gums. He looked ridiculous. "No one says no to this gorgeous face."

That did me in, and I started to laugh. "All right, you got me."

He relaxed his face and flipped off the light. "We'll wait until the bell rings and the hall clears, then we'll take the back way out."

I waited quietly behind him, trying not to hyperventilate at the very idea of skipping school.

In less than two minutes, the bell rang and everyone hurried to their classes. Kai cracked open the door and stuck his head out, looking around to ensure the coast was clear. He waved at me to follow him, and then we shut the door behind us. Just as we reached the small entryway that led to the exit, we heard voices. He grabbed my hand and pulled me the rest of the way out of the building. We ran all the way across the campus and to a spot near the street, where he'd parked his motorcycle.

"What do you do when it gets too cold to ride this thing?" I asked, knowing that winter weather was just weeks away.

He shrugged. "Haven't worked that out yet. I guess I'll buy a car or something."

"With what?" I asked as I climbed on the seat behind him.

"Oh yeah. I need a job." He chuckled.

"Is your entire life plan to have no plan?" It seemed to be the way he operated lately.

"No, I have plans. But the most important parts are still in development." He fired up the engine.

That had me curious. I yelled over the engine. "What are the important parts?"

"Someday you'll see." He didn't say another word.

I held on tight as he sped away from the school and toward the clubhouse.

When we got there, he wasted no time getting me inside. He quickly pulled me into the hall and down past several doors. We reached one on the left, and he opened it, dragging me in behind him. The room was mostly empty, with the exception of a bed, a chair, and a bookshelf. It appeared Kai still had all his belongings in his bag on the floor.

Once the door was shut, I whirled on him. "Why are you shoving me around?"

"Sorry, just trying to get through this without you being seen." He ran a hand through his hair.

"What's the big deal? They think we're dating, right?" Sometimes I didn't understand him.

"Yeah, but . . ." He frowned. "It's just easier if we don't have to explain anything at all."

"And what if they catch me here?" It seemed like we'd better have a cover story.

"We tell them you're skipping school, and we're in here making out."

I pushed a big puff of breath past my lips. "My reputation is not going to survive this, is it?"

"I'll do my best to make it right. I promise."

I needed to focus. "Let's just get this done. What did you find?"

He pulled the paper from his pocket and sat on the bed. "Here's a membership list from when Baxter was here. There was a member who went by Doc."

Well, that was something. "Any other info on him?"

"From what I could find, it looks like he and Baxter were banished from the club at the same time."

"Banished?" That had an ominous sound.

"Yes, when you screw up big around here, you don't just get kicked out. Banishment is the merciful punishment. Dead is the other option." He looked back down at the sheet of paper in his hand. "Baxter and Doc were doing something they shouldn't have. It's the only way they would have been banished."

I tried to imagine what would have been even beyond SIN's code of ethics.

"Miranda, there's a chance your dad didn't run out on you. He may have been forced to leave. Banishment makes life tough here in Havenwood Falls. The smart thing is to move on and start a life somewhere else, if you aren't already forced into it."

I gave that some thought. "Really? Then maybe it wasn't because he didn't want us?"

Kai shrugged. "It's possible. I'm not saying that's the absolute truth. He could still be a total scumbag, but it's possible."

"I need to find him, Kai. I have to know what really happened. I have to let him know that mom is sick." The need to find him felt more urgent than ever.

He nodded. "We will."

"How? How do we find someone who was banished?" It felt kind of hopeless.

"We ask for help." He stared at the paper in his hand.

"Who? The club?" That still sounded like a horrible idea. What if they decided Kai was a traitor for helping me and they banished him?

"We don't know until we ask, right?" His face appeared sure, but his voice was less confident. "I'll talk it over with Monte. He'll tell me straight up if it's a bad idea."

I felt a little better knowing he'd check first, although asking a lesser member of the club seemed just as scary. "When this is all out in the open, will they be mad that we lied about dating?"

Kai drew his brows together. "I think we need to keep that one going. There's no reason they need to know about that. As far as they know, I'm helping my girlfriend find info on her dad and Doc to save her mom. I think that would make sense to them."

I nodded. "Yeah, I guess you're right. It'd be hard to understand why you'd go through all of this for some random girl." It hit me then. Why was he going through all of this for me? I knew he covered for me at first, but he had gone above and beyond at this point.

He studied the paper while I studied him, allowing myself to piece together all I'd learned about Kai in the last few days. It was obvious he wasn't who I once thought he was. There was a depth to him that I didn't see until I really got to know him. And I'd bet even then he had willingly opened up and let me see those vulnerabilities.

"What are you looking at?" He looked at the front of his shirt, ensuring there was nothing on it.

"You," I said softly. "I owe you an apology."

"No, you really don't." He adjusted the way he was sitting so he could face me better.

"I do. When we were at the gazebo Saturday, I said some unkind things about you. You said I didn't know what I was talking about." I sighed. "You were right. I didn't understand at all. I'm sorry."

He shrugged. "Honestly, it's okay. It's my fault people see me as a spoiled snobby elitist. That whole act is how I've been trained to behave." He chuckled. "It's not really who I am, or who I want to be. I'm not exactly an extrovert by nature."

I smiled. "You sure have everyone fooled. Maybe you should go into acting?"

He shook his head. "That'd probably be my worst nightmare. The jerk act has kept a lot of people at arm's length, which I like, for the most part. Sadly, it's kept the people I wanted to get to know better away from me as well." His eyes met mine, and there was something there that made my heart leap in my chest.

I felt that increasingly familiar heat rise in my cheeks. "I—"

A loud commotion down the hall halted anything else I might have said. Kai jumped up and ran to his door, cracking it open enough that he could see what was happening. He turned to face me. "It's just the guys. Looks like they're celebrating something, but they're coming this way."

He quickly shut the door and ran to the bed. He shoved the paper behind me and then pushed me on top of it. The next thing I knew, he was half on top of me, his face not even an inch from mine.

"They're coming," he whispered. "They can't find the paper until I talk to Monte."

"Then I guess we need to give them a show," I murmured. I pulled his head down to mine, and our lips connected. A jolt of exhilaration ran through me as he relaxed against me. I tried to keep my senses about me and listen for whomever was coming down the hall, but I was slowly disappearing into one of the most amazing kisses I'd ever experienced. His lips moved over mine as his hands began to roam down my torso. I moaned into his mouth and ran my fingers through his hair. Kai deepened the kiss.

The door flew open and banged against the wall, but I was so lost in the feelings Kai was stirring that I didn't let it concern me. A voice said, "Oops! Sorry, dude!" Then a loud laugh was followed by the door closing and the distant yell of "Kai's gettin' him some!"

I pulled away just a little, and Kai did the same. He stared down at me, his breathing fast and erratic.

I took a deep breath. "Do you think we convinced them?"

He continued to look down at me. "You sure convinced me."

There was no smirk or attitude in his statement. He actually looked confused.

"Oh, well. I guess I'm getting better at this." I didn't think it was smart to admit that I was kissing him because I wanted to. Not if he didn't feel the same.

He sat up and finger-combed his hair. He cleared his throat a couple of times, then stood.

"Kai, are you okay?"

"Yeah, I'm fine. I just need . . . a minute." His voice was raspy, and I worried I'd upset him.

"Did I do something wrong?" He wouldn't even look at me.

"No," he said quickly. "You were perfect. Absolutely perfect." He groaned. "And if you keep being so perfect, you are gonna be the death of me."

CHAPTER 10

*K*ai and I grabbed lunch at Napoli's, looking over the list for any other possible clues. Nothing of note stood out. He gave me the impression he didn't want to talk about kissing, so I didn't bring it up again. I was nervous about running into my classmates since it was so close to our regular lunch time, but what few students were there only waved and went about their business. He drove me back to the school to get my belongings, then dropped me off at home a little after two p.m. When I walked through the door, Mom was waiting for me.

"Where have you been?" She was angry and looked exhausted.

"What do you mean?" I was going to claim innocence for as long as I could.

"I got a call from Principal Friske. He was worried because you disappeared after second period and never came back." She tapped her foot on the carpet. That was a bad sign.

"I left with Kai." Why not try the truth again? Sort of. I wasn't going to tell her we went to the SIN clubhouse. I wasn't that delusional.

"Why is Kai encouraging you to skip school? This isn't like you at all, Miranda. What is going on with you?" She was obviously disappointed in me.

"I just needed a break. I've been anxious and having a hard time focusing. I'm worried about you . . . I just needed to get away, Mom." I moved to her and wrapped her in a hug. "I'm sorry. I tried to call, but you know how terrible the cell service is here." I felt bad about that lie, but I knew she wouldn't be okay with the real reason I skipped school.

She hugged me back. "Well, anything is better than just running off. Mercy, girl, I was about to go nuts with worry. Next time leave a note, at least."

"I promise I won't do that again." I kissed her cheek. "If I have another problem like that, I'll be sure to keep you in the loop."

"Good. Thank you." She sighed. "We need to discuss your punishment. But for now, let's get something to eat. I'm starving."

A moment later, my world changed. Mom took two steps into the kitchen and collapsed.

"Mom!" I shouted. "Are you okay?"

She didn't respond.

"Oh no!" I grabbed my phone, remembering the emergency number Mom had entered the day before.

"Hello! Dr. Underwood! It's Miranda Saunders. My mom just collapsed. I don't know what to do." I did my best not to cry, but the tears were pushing through every syllable.

"Try to stay calm. Are you at home?" His voice was soothing and was one of the reasons he was such a great doctor. He was also fae and one of the few medical experts in town we could trust with mom's situation.

"Yes," I answered.

"I'll be right there. Meanwhile, make sure she's breathing."

Breathing—another one of those oddities we shared that other vampires didn't have to deal with.

I hung up the phone and crouched next to mom. She was breathing, but it was labored. Silent tears rolled down my face. I couldn't lose her. She was the only family I had. If Mom died . . . I couldn't even finish the thought.

I took her limp hand in mine. "Mom, I don't know if you can hear me, but Dr. Underwood is coming. He's gonna help us. I just need you to hang in there for me, okay? Please don't leave me."

I squeezed her hand, hoping, praying for her to squeeze it back. I needed a sign that she was still with me. I got nothing.

I sat by her side, talking to her, begging her to wake up. As the minutes passed, her breaths became harder to detect.

I heard the front door open, and I turned to see Dr. Underwood rushing toward us, his medical bag in hand. He was wearing jeans and a dark blue button-down shirt that almost matched his eyes. He must have had the day off. I stepped aside as he checked her vital signs.

"She's dehydrated." He opened her eyelids and checked her pupils.

"She was throwing up a lot yesterday," I informed him.

"She didn't tell you to call me?" He seemed surprised and ran a hand through his salt-and-pepper hair.

"No, she said she just needed to sleep a little. She'd been running a fever, too. It broke late last night." I clasped my hands together, needing to keep them occupied so I wouldn't give in to the urge to grab her and hold on.

"I need to get her to the med center." His words were calm but they created a panic in my chest.

"Is she going to be okay?"

"We'll take good care of her." He dialed a number and went outside.

I kneeled next to Mom and hugged her. "You have to get better. I'm going to find out what's going on, Mom. I promise. I don't care what it takes."

Within minutes, two men with a stretcher arrived, and they loaded Mom into an ambulance. I stood at the door watching as they secured her inside and began running vitals.

"Miranda, I'll call you as soon as we have things set up. I have someone preparing a private room for her right now. I know this is unusual, but this isn't a usual situation. Do you have someone who can be with you or somewhere you can go?"

Zoey's family would take me in without question. But oddly enough, Zoey wasn't who I wanted to see. I wanted to call Kai. "Yes, I'll be fine. I'll have my cell on me when you're ready."

He nodded, got in his car, and followed the ambulance down the street.

~

I PULLED up in front of the SIN clubhouse and parked Mom's car. Kai's motorcycle was two spots down, so I knew he was there. I wasn't sure if I should knock or just walk in. I opted for walking in. I pushed open the door and entered the clubhouse. Crusher was just about to enter the hallway.

"Crusher, hi. Have you seen Kai?" I tried to seem confident, as if I belonged there.

He jerked his thumb in the direction of a door toward the back of the room. "He's in the conference room." Then he disappeared down the hall.

I hurried to the door, once again not sure how to proceed. I was about to knock when I realized the door was partially open. I could hear Kai and a voice I didn't recognize talking inside.

"This is the last address I had for Doc. We've been trying to keep tabs on him for years, to make sure he doesn't cause trouble for us again. But I can't guarantee it's current. He's a crafty creature, and he's slipped our grasp a few times." The voice was deep and clear.

"Thanks, I'll check it out." I smiled when I heard Kai's voice.

"I need to warn you, Kai. Doc is dangerous. You'll need to be on your guard. He did some unspeakable things back in the day." I frowned at that bit of news from the unknown voice.

"All the info about him is in here?" Kai's voice was determined.

"All that we know."

Kai coughed. "Holy crap."

"Yeah, it's bad." A brief pause, then I heard, "Are you going to tell the little lady?"

"I guess I have to." Kai chuckled. "Since she's eavesdropping outside the door."

"But otherwise you would have kept it from me?" I pushed open the door. "And I wasn't eavesdropping, I was just trying not to interrupt."

The man standing next to Kai was huge. One glance at his jeans, leathers, and tattoos, and I recognized him as one of the bikers that passed me on my way to school the day I found the photo of my mother and Baxter. He tilted his head at me slightly, and his sandy hair fell over his dark sunglasses just a bit.

Monte had been quietly standing near the back of the room. At this point, he grabbed his stomach and laughed. "Oh, you are so whipped, bruh!"

Kai looked at the larger man. "Liam, this is Miranda."

Liam nodded his head in my direction, and I smiled in return.

Kai held his hands up, one of which contained an envelope. "Miranda, I wasn't going to keep this from you."

I glared at him. "So if I hadn't been standing here, you'd have told me everything?"

He sighed. "Yes . . . eventually."

"Sounds a little sketchy to me," Monte interjected.

Kai turned to scowl at him. "Not. Helping."

Liam smiled at me. "Keep him in line, sweetheart. Don't let him do anything stupid."

Kai rolled his eyes and stuffed the envelope in his back pocket.

Monte and Liam walked past me and out the door.

"Good luck, you two." Liam turned and faced me. "Be extra careful, Miranda. If you meet Doc, don't tell him you're Sade's daughter. Not that he won't figure it out on his own, if his memory is intact. You might be careful what you tell Baxter, as well. At least until you're sure he's on your side."

I nodded. "I will. Thank you."

He looked at Kai. "We have your back."

Kai slapped his palm against Liam's. "Thanks man. We appreciate it."

My cell phone rang. "Sorry, I need to take this." I turned away from them and answered it. "Hello?"

When I looked up, Liam had disappeared out the front door.

Dr. Underwood was on the other end. "We have her in a room and stable. When you're ready, go to the front desk and ask for me. I'll come get you."

"Okay, thank you. Be there soon."

I hung up, and for a moment had forgotten my frustration with Kai.

He stepped closer. "What's wrong?"

I looked up, fighting the urge to cry yet again. "Mom collapsed. She's in the hospital."

He pulled me into his arms, and I buried my face in his chest.

"I'm so sorry." He kissed the top of my head. "Is she at the medical center?"

I nodded, then pulled back to look at him. "Dr. Underwood put her in a special room. That was him on the phone. He said we could come see her now."

"We?" Kai asked.

"Well, if you want to go with me. You don't have to."

He didn't respond.

"I don't really want to do this alone, but I can call Zoey if you—"

He cut me off. "No, I want to go. I'm just surprised you want me there."

"I do." I needed him there, no matter how annoyed I was with him at times. He'd become important to me. I could deny it to myself all I wanted, but it didn't make it any less true.

"Let's go see her then." He put his hand on my lower back and guided me out of the club.

I held up the key fob to my mom's red Hyundai and pushed the unlock button. It beeped, and the lights flashed. "I'm driving this time."

"After you." He followed me to the car.

We drove the short trip to the hospital in silence. I wanted to see her so badly, but I was also terrified of what I might find. Once we reached the front desk, I did as Dr. Underwood instructed, and he joined us within minutes.

"Miranda, I want to prepare you for what you're going to see." He put a hand on my shoulder as we stopped outside an unmarked room. "It looks pretty scary, and honestly we don't yet know what's going on, but I have hope we can figure it out."

I nodded, and he opened the door to the room. I grasped Kai's hand as we walked in side by side.

Mom lay there, still as a stone, tubes and wires seeming to come from everywhere. A machine next to her monitored her heartbeat and oxygen levels, which again was a weird thing to witness with a vampire. I walked to the side of the bed and touched her arm. "Is she breathing on her own?"

"Thankfully, yes," Dr. Underwood said. "That being said, you need to know that she hasn't woken up yet."

My eyes flew to his face. "Is she in a coma?"

"We aren't ready to call it that just yet. We're still running some tests." He scratched his head. "It's odd. She's having some strangely . . . mammal-like medical issues."

"Mammal-like?" What did that even mean? It made no sense at all.

"Yes, like her blood pressure dropping rapidly, then spiking. Heart palpations. Hypoglycemia. Very erratic stuff. It doesn't make sense."

I frowned and looked at Kai. "Do vampires have blood pressure?"

He shrugged. "I don't. Our circulatory systems work differently than humans'."

"We are doing all we can to ensure she's getting the best care. You are welcome to stay if you like. There's a recliner in the corner if you'd like to rest. The kitchen just closed, but I guess that doesn't matter much to either of you. I'll let the front desk know you are allowed to come and go as you need to. As before, I'll contact you if I learn anything new." Dr. Underwood looked at my mom's chart one last time and left the room.

Kai and I sat quietly by her bedside for the next hour, the beep of the monitors the only sound breaking the silence. I held Mom's hand as Kai clasped my other hand in his. It was comforting to have him there with me. He turned out to be the strength that was holding me upright when it felt like my whole world had collapsed. I laid my head on the bed and closed my eyes, trying to clear my mind of any worries. I just wanted to think happy, healing thoughts and send them to her. I hoped that somehow they'd leave my mind and enter her body.

My eyes closed, and suddenly I found myself surrounded by a fog. I was running through a forest. I was being chased, but I couldn't see what was chasing me. I looked behind me, but all I could see were glowing red eyes. Terror struck me as I continued to flee, looking for anything I could use as a weapon, should I need to fight. Then the screaming began. That faint sound of misery and fear welling up from somewhere ahead. I battled the urge to turn around, now caught between whatever was screaming and whatever was chasing me. The voice ahead was getting louder, and it caused my head to ache. I felt something behind me, and there was an odd odor in the air. I turned in time to see the eyes right behind me.

I woke with a start. I must have been exhausted, as sunlight was beginning to peek around the window shades. I'd slept all night. I heard the faint sound of Kai's voice, but didn't see him in the room. The door was ajar, and when I walked over, I saw him pacing the hallway just outside as he talked on his cell phone.

I stepped out and leaned against the door jamb. I gave him a little wave.

He waved back, but walked farther away, still talking in hushed tones. Something was up.

I went back into the room and checked on Mom. Her condition appeared to be the same. I leaned over and kissed her cheek, then brushed some stray hairs from her forehead. That's when I noticed something odd. Mom's usually shiny blond hair, very much like my own, was starting to turn gray. I ran the strands through my fingers.

"What is happening?" I whispered.

I pulled the chair closer to the head of the bed and sat back down. I studied her face. Her perfect skin was now showing the beginning of crow's feet. Her normally full lips were thinner and chapped. I picked up her hand and inspected it closely. The skin seemed more translucent, and her wrist felt fragile.

I stood up and rushed to the door just in time to run into Kai. He looked angry.

"Kai, I think I know what's happening. At least part of it," I blurted out.

He frowned. "What do you mean?"

"With mom. I think she's aging. Quickly."

Kai pushed me back into the hospital room and shut the door. "It's a little more complicated than that."

"More complicated than an immortal aging rapidly?" I frowned at him. "And how do you know it's more complicated?"

"I just got off the phone with Liam. I read something in that information he gave me that I wasn't sure I understood, so I called him to verify." He sat down in the recliner and put his head in his hands. "This is bad."

I pulled the other chair close to him and sat down. "What are you talking about?" The terror I was feeling was steadily coming through in my voice.

Kai clasped my hands in his. "Okay, so you are partially right. Your mom is likely aging rapidly." He shook his head. "We have to find this Doc guy and find a way to make him fix this."

"Does he know what's happening?" At this point, I was willing to take answers from anyone.

Kai's anger was barely controlled. "According to Liam, he's the reason it's happening."

CHAPTER 11

*D*r. Underwood walked into Mom's room just as I finished scanning the information Kai had on Doc and Baxter.

I looked at Kai. "Can this be reversed?"

"I don't know, but Dr. Underwood might."

The doctor looked up at the mention of his name. "What was that?"

"We think we know part of the problem." I said. "According to records we got from . . . a reliable source, my father was mixed up with an Unseelie fae who went by the nickname of Doc."

Dr. Underwood frowned. "Yeah, I know of him. He considered himself some sort of a scientist back when I knew him. The guy wasn't all there."

"He and my father were dealing. My dad didn't know that Doc had been messing with the chemical composition of the drugs. Doc thought addicts were useless sores on society, so he decided he would attempt to transform the poor souls into other creatures. Creatures that would look to him as their god."

Dr. Underwood shook his head. "Sounds like him. He had some crazy ideas."

"My mom and dad were addicts back then, Dr. Underwood." It

was hard to admit that out loud. I knew my mother would hate her past being brought back out into the open.

He glanced at the frail shell of a woman slipping away from us. My proud, beautiful mother. "I'd heard the rumors, but I didn't know if they were true."

"She beat her addiction when she found out she was expecting me."

I watched him putting the pieces together in his mind. "I see. This may explain a lot."

"It seems that way," I said.

Kai spoke then. "If we find Doc and haul him back here, can you make him fix this?"

"I don't know. I can try. But he's not going to be easy to persuade. And he's probably dangerous." Dr. Underwood checked mom's pupils. "Be very careful. Get help to do this, and make sure you're prepared, but do what you need to do as soon as you can."

Kai nodded, grabbed his phone, and went out into the hall again.

I moved to Mom's side and leaned over her. "Mom, I'll be back soon. We're gonna go get help." I kissed her forehead and left the room to find Kai.

He was standing near the door, the phone to his ear. "Yes, got it. Thank you. I owe you one." He hung up and shoved the cell in his pocket. "Let's go."

"Where?" I asked, as Kai led me to Mom's car. I'd just pulled my keys from my pocket when he swiped them from my hand.

"I'm driving."

I didn't argue as we buckled in. I was too upset to drive. "Where are we going?"

"We're meeting your dad." He put the car in reverse and quickly backed out of the parking spot.

"What?" I squeaked. "You found him?"

"Sort of." Kai pulled onto the street, squealing the tires. "Agatha Temple did a location spell for me."

I was confused. "The chubby, dark-haired woman who drives the shuttle?"

He nodded.

"I didn't even know she was a witch." There was so much I didn't yet know about our little town.

"She's pretty chill about it."

"When did she do this? What did she find?"

"While you were sleeping, I asked her to see if she could do it. I sent her a picture of your picture, since we had nothing else to go on. I didn't even think it'd work since you usually need a personal item of the person you're looking for, but we didn't have anything to lose by trying. And Agatha's good." He pulled the photo out of his pocket and handed it to me. "I took it while you were asleep. Anyway, Baxter is living in a cabin about fifty miles from here."

He pointed the car west and steered us down County Road 13.

"He's only been fifty miles away? All this time?" I couldn't believe what I was hearing. "Why didn't he check on us? Call? Write a freakin' letter? He had twenty-eight days before the memory spell kicked in. He could have at least let mom know what was going on before he forgot about us completely."

Kai focused on the road. "He couldn't come back, so maybe he felt like it was pointless."

"Pointless?" I could feel my anger rising. I couldn't direct it all at Baxter. He was only part of the reason we were in this mess. Mom was partially responsible, and Doc carried the biggest load of the blame. It was Doc I wanted to scream at and throttle.

The more I thought about it, the angrier I got. I started to literally see red. I closed my eyes and placed the palms of my hands over my eyelids. My head began to hurt.

"Are you okay?" Kai's voice sounded distant and slightly muffled over the almost deafening sound of screaming I heard in my ears. I didn't understand what was happening or what I was feeling, and I worried that some of the things in my dreams were pushing through to reality, but intuition told me I needed to calm down.

I blew out a shaky breath and looked at him. "Yeah, I'm just . . . I've never been so angry in all of my life." I balled my hands into fists.

"Really?" His lips pulled to one side. "Huh. I would have thought I'd made you furious at least a time or two."

I smiled. "You've come really close."

The closer we got to the cabin, the antsier I became. I couldn't keep from tapping my foot on the floorboard or drumming my fingers on the armrest. I could tell Kai wanted to say something, but he didn't, and I appreciated his understanding. I was sure my one-man-band act had to be annoying.

We pulled up to a small gravel road, and Kai turned and followed it all the way to a dead end. Sitting before us was a modest cabin. It looked no bigger than what most would consider a hunting shack. It was surrounded by trees, and hidden well. Kai turned off the engine, and we sat quietly for a moment, just staring at the dark wooden door. It was a typical log-cabin-style build and looked like it probably started as one of those do-it-yourself kits.

"Whenever you're ready." He didn't want to rush me, even though we really needed to hurry.

"No time like the present," I muttered.

We opened the car doors and stepped out, when the cabin door opened and a middle-aged man with a shotgun stepped forward. He pointed the barrel directly at us.

"You've got the wrong house, kids. Turn around and go back the way you came." His voice was raspy and low.

It was Baxter. He looked older, and I assumed he was aging, similar to my mother, but his features were distinct. His blond hair was shaggy, and he was thinner than the man in the photo. He wore a faded pair of jeans, black button-up shirt with the sleeves rolled up to the elbow, boots, and the tattered cowboy hat he wore in the picture.

"Are you Baxter Morrison?" I asked.

He lowered the gun slightly. "I don't know anyone by that name."

He wanted to play dumb? Fine. "Do you know a Sade Saunders?"

"Nope," he answered.

"Can we just speak with you for a few minutes?" Kai asked.

"No need. We have nothing to say to each other." He raised the gun again and continued to point it in our direction.

"I'd say we do," said Kai. "And that gun isn't gonna do jack to us, because we're vampires."

Baxter narrowed his eyes at Kai.

"But better than that," continued Kai, "this beautiful young woman is your daughter. You wouldn't want to shoot up your own baby girl, now would you?"

Baxter scoffed. "Vampires don't procreate."

"Our kind doesn't. Not normally. But you're not normal, are you, Baxter?" Kai took a step forward. "You're aging, and you're sick. Just like Miranda's mother."

"Miranda?" Baxter lowered the gun and slowly walked down the steps. He looked me over slowly. "Your name is Miranda?"

I nodded.

"That was my mother's name, a long, long time ago." The hard lines of his face softened just a bit.

"I guess that's why Mom chose the name." I wasn't sure why she'd chosen it. I'd never thought to ask, but I'd run with that if it would get him to listen to us.

He frowned. "I don't understand any of this." He looked around. "Hurry. Get inside."

He shooed us up the steps and inside the cabin. When he locked the door behind him, I noticed odd symbols painted on the door and other spots inside the cabin walls.

"What are all these?" I took a closer look at one.

Baxter placed his gun to the side of the door. "Those are wards to keep undesirables out."

"Undesirables?" Kai asked.

"Fae," he answered. Then he pointed to iron hanging on the walls. "Iron helps, too."

Kai and I looked at each other.

Kai spoke first. "You wouldn't be avoiding a specific fae, would you? One called Doc?"

Baxter stiffened. "What do you know about Doc?"

I decided to take over. "We know that he likes to play god. We know that he was experimenting with a combination of drugs, DNA, and magic. We know that you and my mother were addicts and ended up with Doc's drugs in your system. So he cursed the drugs you were stealing. In the meantime, it altered your DNA just enough that you got my vampire mother pregnant. Then you and Doc got caught by the leader of your motorcycle club and were banished from Havenwood Falls."

He pulled his eyebrows together in a disbelieving expression. "Havenwood Falls? Never heard of it."

"That's because once you left town, the memory spell slowly wiped all that from your mind," Kai answered.

Baxter rubbed his chin. "I don't know if I believe any of this."

"Can you account for how you got here? In this cabin? Hiding from Doc?" I asked.

He looked around. "Actually, no. All I recall is that Doc was after me. He kept saying I took something from him and I ruined everything, but I didn't know what he was talking about. After a few weeks, I'm not sure he knew what he was talking about either. He kept vowing revenge, though. I've been battling the little jerk ever since." He sighed. "But I'm getting too weak to keep it up."

I passed the photo I carried to him. "That's you, standing next to my mother."

He studied the photo. "She does kind of look familiar." He raised his eyes to mine. "You look a lot like her."

I nodded and smiled.

"We need to find Doc," Kai said. "He knows how to heal Miranda's mother . . . and you."

Baxter looked at Kai. "You think so?"

He passed the picture back to me.

"We know so," I said.

"He's crazy. And dangerous. Do you know what you're getting into here?" he asked.

We both nodded.

"Okay then, what's your plan?" Baxter was warming up to us.

Kai ticked the points off on his fingers as he spoke. "We need to lure Doc back into Havenwood Falls. Once he's there, we have people that can handle him. They'll figure out the cure, you and Sade can get better, and you won't have to worry about Doc ever again."

Baxter thought on it for a moment. "What have I got to lose? If I stay here, I'll eventually die anyway. Might as well take a chance or go out in a blaze of glory."

Kai smiled. "I like your style."

I smacked Kai's arm with the back of my hand.

"Thank you," I said to Baxter. "I can't tell you how much this means to me."

He gave me a small smile. "No problem." He tipped his old hat in my direction. "Just glad I'm useful for a change."

WE MAPPED out the plan for drawing Doc out, which included making a few calls back home. We ensured the right people were prepared for plan A, plan B, and plan C. We'd get Doc there one way or another. Plan A was that Kai would drive my mom's car back to Havenwood Falls, and I'd ride with Baxter in his truck as he followed Kai. I knew that once Baxter got into town, his memories would likely start to return. He might change his mind, so I wanted to be with him when we crossed the town's border. If he flaked out on us, I was determined to bring him back to reason. Kai wasn't happy about leaving me alone with Baxter, but I wasn't budging on the issue.

"It could be dangerous, Miranda. Doc could attack before we get home." Kai gripped my shoulders.

"It's possible. And if he does, that's what plan B is for. I'll be there to protect Baxter, and our friends will help us get him home safely," I countered.

"What if you get hurt?" Kai's frustration was loud and clear.

"I won't. You'll be right in front of me. It'll be fine." I smiled up at him, and he rolled his eyes.

I crossed mine. "C'mon. No one can say no to this face." I mimicked the way he'd said those very words to me the day before.

He smirked, but didn't say anything.

"Really. I've got this. What can I do to convince you to trust me?"

He stared at me for a moment, then stepped closer. "Kiss me."

My goofy grin faded. "What?"

"Kiss me. I can't let you out of my sight until I've had one sincere, heartfelt kiss from you. One I know, without a doubt, you really mean." He didn't smile, and there was no teasing tone in his voice.

"Is this one of your practical jokes? Because it's not funny."

He shook his head.

"You really want to kiss me?" I thought I might be dreaming.

He framed my face with his hands, one thumb softly stroking my cheek. "I do. I've wanted to ask you out for years. And if there is any chance that this is the last time I might have to tell you how much I care about you, I'm not wasting it."

He pressed his lips to mine, and this time I didn't allow my mind to think up horrible scenarios or wonder what his motives might be. I just kissed him back and enjoyed knowing that it was something we both wanted.

He pulled back and looked into my eyes. "When this is over, we need to talk."

I nodded. "Sure."

He lowered his hands and took one of mine in his. "Be careful." He raised my hand to his lips and kissed it. He dropped it as he backed away and got into the car.

Behind me, Baxter started up his truck. "Ready?"

I turned. "Ready as I'll ever be," I said. "Let's set the hook."

CHAPTER 12

$\mathcal{W}$e followed Kai with only a few car lengths between us. It was close enough that he wouldn't lose us, but far enough that if Doc were to strike, Kai wouldn't get caught in the crossfire. Baxter looked relaxed as he drove, but every now and then, I caught him checking his mirrors and monitoring the landscape around us. I didn't know if he sensed something, but I did. It was that feeling I'd been fighting since this all began. The ominous apprehension was stronger than ever.

We were only about two miles outside of town when the truck was hit with a blast of something invisible. The force felt like what I'd imagine a cannonball would feel like if it'd hit us broadside. For a brief moment, I saw Baxter's arm shoot out toward me in an effort to protect me, much like my mother did when I was little. Then the world around us spun out of control, with trees and mountainsides blurring together before my vision. The sickening sound of metal meeting something solid filled my ears as we landed hard in a ditch.

Baxter reached over and touched my arm. "Are you okay?"

"Yeah. What was that?" I sat up, attempting to pull the too-tight seatbelt away from my chest.

"I'm not sure." Baxter tried to open his door, but it wouldn't budge. "My door's jammed." He unbuckled his seatbelt and rolled down the window. After quickly poking his head out to look at the door, he turned to me. "There's a huge dent in my door."

I looked ahead on the highway to see Kai turning around. I tried not to panic, but whatever hit us might hit Kai next. He needed to keep going.

Another blast hit the truck from the front and shook it violently. I screamed as the windshield cracked and caved in, while the side windows shattered and littered the inside of the cab with small pebble-like glass. I could feel fragments of it clinging to my hair.

It was then that I heard a menacing male voice. "I knew you couldn't hide from me forever, Baxter."

I looked up to see a youngish-looking man with dark hair and dark eyes walking toward us in the middle of the highway. He was decked out in all black clothing, right down to his boots.

I looked past him and couldn't see Kai anymore. I tried not to panic. *What had he done with Kai?* I tugged on my seatbelt, but it wouldn't budge.

Baxter reached across and handed me a knife. "Here, cut the strap."

I did as he instructed and moved closer to him.

"We may be in a pickle here. He's a lot stronger than me. I don't know what you can do, Miranda. Let's hope we can hold out until Kai can get help." Baxter rubbed his temples.

"Are you okay? Did you hit your head?" I worried he might have a concussion.

"No, it's just . . . I'm getting these weird flashbacks."

"The memories. They're starting to return." I gasped. "That means Doc's probably are too. We have to get out of here."

I tried to open my door, but it was stuck as well. I turned my back to Baxter. "I'm gonna brace myself against you. Push against me."

He leaned himself into my back, and I kicked the door as hard as I could. It gave way just a little, but not enough to open.

"Let's try again," I said through labored breaths.

Baxter leaned in again, and I adjusted myself to where I could kick with both feet. This time the door shot off its hinges. I grabbed Baxter's hand. "Let's go!"

"Where are we going?" he said, as he grabbed the small bag from the floorboard and scooted toward the passenger door.

"Plan B. We're going to play a little game of hide-and-seek with Doc." I pulled out my phone and hit the pre-programmed text message I had set to go. All it said was "Plan B." It went out to several friends. They all knew what to do.

We ran just a few feet into the trees when we heard Doc yell for us. "Do you really think you can hide from me among a few trees?"

He laughed, and it echoed around us.

If we could just make it a little farther, I knew a great hiding spot to kill the time we needed. We heard branches break behind us, and a sound that roared like a mighty wind rushed to meet our backsides. We hit the ground and covered our heads as we felt another blast of invisible energy move over us. It came a little too close for comfort.

I could see the tree we needed. It was just across a small clearing. We'd have to make a run for it.

"Baxter, we'll have to run for that tree. The one with the huge trunk. Do you see it?"

Baxter was staring at me. "You look just like her. I can't believe it."

I nodded. "We can talk later. Right now we have to focus on not dying."

He looked at the tree and then back to where we thought Doc was. "I'm ready."

"Go," I urged.

We sprinted across the open space, branches and leaves crunching beneath our feet. We'd just made it when we heard Doc again. "I can sense you. No matter where you hide, I'll find you. Why don't you make this easier on all of us and just give up?"

We crouched behind the large tree and opened the small bag we'd brought along. I grabbed an iron rod and chain. Baxter grabbed an iron dagger.

"Stay here. My friend Conrad will be along soon to get you. He'll take you to Mom." I paused. "Don't freak out if he's naked. He's a dragon and probably didn't bring any clothes with him for shifting to human and back."

He nodded, but looked a little concerned by that. He reached for me. "But what about you?"

"I'll be fine. I'll distract Doc until you're safe. Then we'll get him into town so he can be dealt with." I tried to sound more confident than I felt. Sure I was a vampire, although not exactly like the others. But I'd never had to fully put my skills to the test.

Baxter frowned. "Be careful, Miranda. I don't want to lose you now that I've found you."

"You won't. Now stay down and quiet."

I knew Conrad was close. I could smell the pungent odor of sulfur that followed him when he was in his lava dragon form. He was currently using his camouflage, or we could have easily picked him out among the trees surrounding us.

Sulfur. I now recognized the smell from my dream. Was the thing chasing me a lava dragon? I didn't have time to analyze that, so I filed it away to examine later.

I glanced down at the new message on my cell phone. The SIN club found the truck and were almost in position. Jetta was looking for Kai. It was time.

I stepped out from behind the tree. "Doc, how about we talk? I don't think all this violence is really doing anyone any good."

"Oh, I don't know," he said, his voice still seeming to come from every direction. "I'm rather enjoying it."

"It's a waste of your time. Baxter is already gone. He's safe in Havenwood Falls. Of course, you could always go after him." I smiled.

"Do you think I'm stupid? I know what happens if I step foot in that town again. Liam doesn't forgive or forget. I have Baxter to thank for that. But you know all that, don't you, Sade?"

I chuckled. He thought I was my mother. Which meant he didn't know she was sick. I tried to use that to my advantage.

I tried to mimic something my mother would say. "Yes, we know all about the mess you made."

"I was creating!" he bellowed.

"You were playing with things you shouldn't have," I yelled back.

He laughed. "Want to know a secret? I still am."

He stepped out into the clearing. I could see him well now. His nose was sharp, and his features were angled. His black eyes narrowed. "There's something different about you, Sade. I wonder what it is." He stepped closer.

"Stay where you are. You are surrounded, and I suggest you cooperate if you want to live."

He shrugged. "You won't touch me."

"And why is that?" I asked.

"Because I have a hostage." He reached out and pulled Kai out of thin air.

"Miranda, don't do anything he says!" Kai choked out.

"Miranda?" Doc replied. "So you aren't Sade, yet you look very much like her." He studied me a moment, then his face lit up. "I did it, didn't I? You are one of my creations!"

"Let Kai go," I demanded.

He shook his head. "Oh no. That's not going to happen. Not when you have me boxed in like this. I need leverage."

He must have sensed everyone I'd called in, despite any spells or cloaking abilities.

"If I tell them to leave, will you let Kai go?"

Doc thought about that a moment. "I'll need one more thing."

"And what is that?" I asked.

"You," he stated.

"No!" yelled Kai.

Doc hissed at Kai. "Shut up."

"I'll make you a deal," I said. "My friends back off, and you let Kai go. Then it's just you and me. If you can catch me, I'll go with you. No arguments. But if I catch you first, you go with me and help me find a cure for Baxter's and Sade's sickness."

Doc shook his head. "Oh my. Sade's sick too? Such a shame."

"Do we have a bet?" I was working to hold my temper.

He smiled. "We do indeed."

Kai yelled. "What are you doing?"

93

"I'm doing what I have to, to save the people I love." I hoped he caught what I was saying. I wanted him to know that he was included in that group.

Jetta uncloaked herself, her twenty-foot-tall stature an impressive figure, even among the tallest trees in the forest. Her bluish-white scales reflected the light as she moved toward us. Her large blue eyes narrowed as she bent her head lower to the ground, getting a closer at Kai and Doc. Doc stepped back, but pushed Kai in her direction. "Take him, dragon. Get him out of here. This is now between Miranda and me."

Kai pleaded with me. "Miranda, please . . . don't. You don't understand—"

Doc snapped his fingers and cut off Kai's voice. "Quiet, boy. I'm tired of hearing you talk."

"It'll be okay, Kai. I promise." I hoped my voice didn't betray the doubts that came with such a flimsy promise.

Jetta vanished with Kai. Conrad was long gone with Baxter. Most of the SIN club had left, but Liam and Savage had stayed behind. I couldn't see them, but somehow, I knew they were there. Doc didn't say anything, so I didn't know if he sensed them or not. He had a crazed look on his face and was starting to babble to himself. I was suddenly very thankful I wasn't doing this alone. This man was truly mad.

"So," he said. "Do you want me to give you a head start?"

I shrugged. "I was going to give you one."

He pointed a finger at me and laughed. "You are a sassy one."

"Oh, you have no idea," I said, my words laced with venom.

"Well . . ." He looked at his hands, and I took that moment to run, the iron weapons firmly in hand. I ran faster than I'd ever run before. Hopping over logs and dodging low-hanging limbs, I managed to avoid crashing while keeping up a decent rate of speed. My plan was to circle around and get behind him. I still sensed Liam and Savage. They were alongside of me, keeping up with me, but far enough away that they were outside the hearing of most creatures. I couldn't hear them. I felt them. However it was happening, I wasn't going to complain. It gave us the advantage.

I heard Doc's movements, but it was hard to tell just where he was coming from. He was overconfident and wasn't as cautious as he should have been. That was a flaw I was counting on. I quickly climbed a tree to get a better vantage point, and I saw him moving a couple hundred yards behind me. I stayed perfectly still and waited until he passed me.

I jumped down behind him. "Got ya! I win!" I felt sure it wouldn't be that easy, but I had to try.

He laughed, then flicked his wrist and flung me backwards into a tree. I hit my head and landed in the dirt face first.

"Ow." I pushed myself off the ground, spitting out dirt and leaves. "You dirty cheat."

He chuckled. "I'm Unseelie. What part of that do you not understand, little girl?"

"I don't care if you're the devil himself, you are going back with me," I growled.

I ran toward him, and he almost dodged me, but my fingertips managed to grab his shirt, and I jerked him off his feet. He landed on his knees.

I stood over him. "Now, let's go."

"Fine. You win." I backed up, and he stood, then dusted himself off. He bent to wipe dirt from his knee, and when he rose back up, he produced a dagger. He lunged for me and caught my left shoulder. Pain and blood saturated the area. I grabbed my iron chain and swung it in his direction. It hit his hand, and he dropped the knife. He grimaced as he clutched that hand to his chest.

He smiled, but it was one of pure evil. "I'd hate to have to kill you. As your creator, that'd make me very upset. But if that's what it takes, so be it. I can always dissect you, learn your biology, and make another."

I gritted my teeth. "I will die before I go with you," I hissed.

He pulled out a syringe. "Oh, no. I think you'll cooperate."

At that point Liam and Savage stepped out into the open. "You will not lay a hand on her, Doc."

His eyes went wide. "No. You left."

"Did they?" I taunted.

Then once again he pulled Kai out of thin air.

"Impossible! You already let him go!" I yelled.

He threw my own words back in my face. "Did I?" He shook his head. "No, I let a duplicate of him go, which disintegrated once it got to town. I bet that freaked your dragon friend out." He smiled.

"I'm warning you—"

"No, I'm warning you. I'm calling the shots here. Speaking of shots —" He jabbed the needle into Kai's neck.

"No!" I screamed as Kai hit the forest floor.

Doc laughed, and Kai held his neck as he writhed in pain.

I started to shake, and as before, red clouded my vision. In my peripheral vision I could see mist rolling in around us. The screams I'd heard last time were there, but much louder, as if they were right beside me. Then they morphed into the sound of a heartbeat and blood rushing through a maze of veins. There was a throbbing pulse calling to me, right at the base of a neck nearby.

It was Doc's neck. I saw nothing but the outline of Doc's body and his circulatory system pulsing through him. There was also the faint wisp of something dark hovering within him, but I was unaware of what that might be. All I could focus on was the blood.

I lunged, grasping his head and spinning him in the air. He landed on his back with a thud. The wind had been knocked out of him, and I sat crouched on his chest, making it even harder for him to breathe. I held the iron pipe to his throat. He looked up at me.

"You . . . you . . . your eyes . . . ," he stammered.

A deep, beastly growl escaped my lips, and even to my own ears, it sounded wrong. Then, from somewhere around me, I heard a sorrowful howl. I smelled sulfur again. I assumed it was Liam or Savage. It made sense that hellhounds would have that sulfur scent on them as well.

Kai moaned, and my anger peaked. I pushed Doc's face to the side, smashing his cheek into the dirt. It was then I noticed steam rising from my skin, like waves of heat from the pavement on a hot summer day. I refocused on the pulse that beckoned me. I bit into his neck and drank just enough to make it hurt. When I pulled back, his blood dripped from my fangs. I grabbed his face and made him look at me as I allowed his own blood to land in droplets on his cheek.

"I would love nothing better than to finish feeding on you. And then, when there is nothing left but your desiccated corpse, I would personally drag your soul to Hell." I lowered my face a fraction, so we were nose to nose. "But sadly, your sorry life is needed elsewhere. So we are taking you back to town and you will cooperate. You will fix this mess you created. Or I will hunt you to the ends of the earth and finish what I started."

He nodded, and his mouth moved but no voice came out. I growled at him one last time, and then there was another howl. He promptly passed out.

The iron must have wounded him more than I realized. I stood and wiped my mouth. The blood tasted awful, so I spit out what I could, then ran over to check on Kai. He glanced at me, then closed his eyes.

Liam and Savage moved to Doc and put his arms and legs in iron shackles.

"Are you okay?" I touched Kai's neck at the site of the puncture wound. My vision had quickly returned to normal, for which I was thankful.

"I think so." He groaned. "I have no idea what he jacked me up with, though. I think I might be hallucinating."

"I don't know either, but we'll find out." I helped him to his feet, trying to ignore the pain in my shoulder. I hated that I healed slower than most vampires, but I did take comfort knowing that it would be healed soon. "Where's the car?"

"It's on the other side of that hill. I tried to come at it the back way, but he knew I was there." Kai dusted the grass off his clothes.

"Let's get this jerk in the car." I walked toward the unconscious body of Doc.

Kai looked down at him. "Can we drag him by his feet?" he asked.

I laughed. "He deserves it, but no. We need him to be able to think later."

Liam touched my shoulder. "Are you okay?"

I nodded. "It's sore, but it'll heal."

He shot Savage a look, then the two bikers picked Doc up and carried him through the trees, up the hill, and to Mom's car.

Kai put a gag over his mouth, and they tossed him in the trunk. He sent a text message to Dr. Underwood letting him know we were on our way.

I decided to drive us back just in case Kai had any side effects from the injection. Liam and Savage followed on their motorcycles to assure we didn't have any issues with Doc.

I'd just pulled on to the highway when Kai put his hand on my back.

"Miranda?"

"Yeah?" I answered.

"Are you okay?"

"Yeah, it's healing slowly, but it is healing. It sucks not being a pure vampire like you are." I smiled at him.

"Good, but I mean . . . what happened to you back there? Did I imagine that? Was it the injection?" He sounded concerned.

"Honestly, I'm not sure what happened. But you didn't imagine anything." He couldn't have been more concerned than I was. Some very bizarre things happened to me in that forest, and I wasn't convinced they had anything to do with being a vampire.

CHAPTER 13

Savage split off and went to the club to inform the other
members of the mission's progress, while Liam followed us to
the hospital and parked next to our car.

"We did it!" I said as I got out of the car.

Kai just nodded.

"We sure did." Liam looked at Kai and then back at me. He
studied me a moment, then turned his attention to the trunk. "Well,
let's get this monster inside."

I popped the trunk, and Liam and Kai pulled Doc out. The angry
fae glared at them both. When I walked around to face him, he started
yelling under the gag and tried to get away from me. *I must have really
scared the crap out of him.*

Liam gave me another odd look, then he and Kai dragged Doc
into the hospital.

I sat outside for a few minutes, catching my breath and trying to
think. In a matter of a few hours, I'd met my long lost dad, saved him,
found out the guy I loved cared about me, too, got the bad guy to the
hospital to help heal my sick loved ones, and I had an odd moment in
the forest where something new happened when I fed. What a strange

week this had turned out to be. I'd never been on a vacation, but I was pretty sure I was overdue for one after all this.

I went straight to my mother's room. When I got there, I found Baxter sitting next to her bed, in the same spot as I had the day before. He was holding her hand as tears ran down his face.

He looked up at me. "What's happening?"

"Mom's been having health problems the last several weeks. She passed out yesterday and hasn't woken up since. She's aging quickly, much like you." I sat next to him in the recliner.

"Why is she more advanced than me?" He sniffed.

"We aren't sure," I admitted.

He bowed his head. "Dammit Doc!"

"Do you know exactly what he did to those drugs?" I asked.

Baxter stood and paced. "He sold a lot of different crap. And each drug had a different experiment with it. He thought of himself as a scientist." He chuckled. "More like a mad scientist. He was messing with DNA and all other kinds of biological stuff. Tricking people into shooting it up by mixing it with the drugs."

"What was in the stuff you and Mom took?"

He looked me in the eye. "I'm not completely sure. When he found out I'd been stealing from his supply, he was really angry. Only he didn't tell me right away what he'd been doing, or that he knew. Instead he made the mixture stronger and then cursed it with his dark fae magic. He left it where he knew I'd take it. I swear, I had no idea your mom was using my stash, too."

"Dr. Underwood will figure it out. He's gonna make Doc fix it." I tried to reassure him, although I wasn't so sure myself.

"As far as I know, everyone else he'd experimented on died quick deaths a long time ago. My curse was that I'd suffer slowly. Before the memory spell kicked in and wiped all recollection of Havenwood Falls, I'd planned to just die in that cabin alone, hoping he'd never find out about you and your mother." He sighed. "But you came to me instead." He rubbed his temples. "Do everyone's memories come rushing back so quickly like this? It's killing my head."

I shrugged. "I've heard it's different for everyone. You were protecting us?"

"Yes. He didn't know your mom was using. I found out about her pregnancy about the same time he told me what he'd done. I couldn't risk him learning that his idea of creating a new species might have actually worked, even if it wasn't directly the way he'd planned. He would have taken Sade. He'd have taken you. I couldn't allow that. So I admitted everything to Liam and requested that he banish us both. If I wasn't tempted to come back, then I knew you were safe because Doc wouldn't learn about you."

Knowing my father didn't abandon us, but sacrificed his happiness to protect us instead, was heartbreaking and humbling. "Thank you. I can't imagine how difficult that was."

His voice cracked. "Hardest thing I ever did was walk away from you and your mother."

Dr. Underwood walked in. "It will be a little while before we have answers, but he's cooperating reluctantly. At this time, he swears he can't remember exactly what was in the drugs he gave you, Baxter. He does remember that he cursed them, though. We'll keep working on it."

"Thank you, doctor," I said. "Did you find out what he stuck Kai with?"

He nodded. "It was just rubbing alcohol and a flu virus. Thankfully he isn't human, so it won't hurt him long term. He'll be fine very soon. He just needs to rest."

I shook my head. "I don't know what Doc was thinking."

"He probably wasn't," said Dr. Underwood. "Some things he's still a genius at, like DNA splicing, but the simple, common sense stuff seems to have fled his mind years ago. Otherwise, he'd have known jabbing Kai with that wasn't going to do anything."

Baxter broke into a coughing fit, and I put a hand on his back. "Are you okay?"

He nodded. "Yeah, those are just getting more frequent."

I looked at Dr. Underwood, and he frowned. "I'll be back as soon as I can."

After he left the room, Baxter released a deep sigh. "I don't know what's going to happen, but thank you for bringing me home, Miranda. If I have to die, I'm glad I've gotten a chance to see you first."

"You're not gonna die." I refused to let another tear fall. "It's gonna be fine."

He gave me a tired smile. "Sure."

He looked at Mom, and I could see the love he still had for her. It was as if he'd never left us. And I guess for him, it probably felt as fresh as before he'd forgotten. He hadn't had time to grieve or let his feelings fade. Bitterness hadn't had a chance to set in. For Mom and me, it would take a little time. We had seventeen years to make up for. Eighteen, if we counted Mom going through her entire pregnancy alone and her being a pariah of the vampire community. That one was going to be hard to forgive. But I was sure once she heard the reasoning behind Baxter's disappearance, she'd slowly come around.

He stretched and leaned back in his chair. "I think I'm going to rest a bit. This was an exhausting day."

I glanced at my watch. It was later than I'd realized. I stood up.

"Here, take the recliner. It's more comfortable." I grabbed a blanket from the small dresser on the opposite wall and draped it over him as he settled in. "Get some rest, and I'll be back a little later to see what kind of progress they've made."

He nodded and yawned. Before he closed his eyes, he touched my hand. "Miranda, I'm so proud of you. You've become an amazing woman. Just like your mother."

"Thank you." I patted his hand and left the room, shutting the door firmly behind me. Then I let the emotions hit me. I couldn't count all the times I'd wanted to hear my father say he loved me or that he was proud of me. Many of my friends had fathers cheering them on at events and attending daddy-daughter dances, but I was always the girl who stood alone, not even sure who her father was.

I didn't even bother to wipe the tears as I went in search of Kai.

~

I LOOKED in the waiting area, but Kai wasn't there. So I started asking nurses if he'd been admitted to a room. He wasn't on the admissions list either. It wasn't until I passed Dr. Underwood in the hall again roughly twenty minutes later that I learned Kai had left shortly after we'd arrived.

"He let me examine him, asked me if Doc was secure, and then left with Liam." He checked his clipboard, then looked me over. "Are you okay?"

"It's been a weird day. I think I could use a good meal and a shower." That wasn't my first priority, but it sounded believable.

"Well, do that and get a little rest, too. You know I'll call you as soon as I have anything new." He patted me on the shoulder, then continued down the hall.

I slipped out into the parking lot and went to the car. I'd hoped Kai would have at least left me a note, but there was nothing.

I started the car and took off toward the clubhouse. When I pulled up, Kai was sitting on his motorcycle.

I quickly got out and walked over to him. "Going somewhere?"

He shrugged. "I just thought I'd take a ride and clear my head."

"Want some company?" I smiled.

He didn't return it. "I need a little alone time."

"Oh. I see." I did not see. Something had changed. "Did I do something wrong?"

"No, it's not you. I'm just trying to shake off today's events and relax. Ride off the stress."

"Yeah." I stepped back and leaned against my car. "Well, be safe. Don't drive the death machine too fast." I wanted to give him a smile, but I couldn't make it happen.

He stared at me for a moment. "I'll see you soon, okay?"

"Sure."

He started the motorcycle and pulled away. I watched his taillights disappear into the dark, along with my heart.

"He just needs a little time." Liam walked out of the shadows.

"How long have you been there?" I was a little put off that I didn't notice him there, considering I'd felt his presence earlier in the forest. My mind and emotions were so muddled.

"The whole time." He put his thumbs in his pockets. "He's coming to terms with some things. He'll be okay. And he's in love with you."

"Okay." I didn't know what else to say. I was glad to hear he cared. Liam even said the word love, so I should have been ecstatic, but I didn't understand what he needed to reconcile with.

"He saw you transform in the forest when you subdued Doc. It's not something he expected."

"Transform?" I knew my anger had pushed through at that moment, but I didn't realize there was any physical transformation.

"You didn't change shape, so to speak, but your voice deepened to a beast-like growl and your eyes turned red. You threatened to drag Doc to Hell." He stepped closer, leaning against the car next to me.

"Well, I was really angry. And I did see red, which I didn't think could literally happen. I was so angry. He was hurting people I love."

"You called in mist as a defense mechanism and you howled . . . twice." He grinned.

"Don't be silly. I didn't howl, that was one of you guys. The howling, the sulfur, all of that."

He shook his head. "Nope. It was you."

I was confused. "How could it be me and I not know that?"

He shrugged. "It can feel like an out-of-body experience when you start to shift. You were on the verge, I think."

I looked at him. "What do you think happened to me?"

Liam turned to face me and lowered his sunglasses. This was the first time I'd ever seen his eyes. They were dark with a reddish-orange tint. He pushed them back up his nose. "I wear these because it's dangerous to look into the eyes of a hellhound. Mortals, and some supernatural creatures, see their own death. You showed Doc his fate. The red is probably your version of night vision. Being half vampire, you probably experience things a little differently than I do."

I couldn't quite comprehend what I was hearing. "Are you saying I have similar traits to a hellhound?"

He shook his head. "No, I'm saying you are hellhound and

vampire. You got the vampire DNA from your parents and the hellhound DNA from . . ." He gestured to the club. "Likely one of us. Doc was grabbing samples from everyone right under our noses. Whatever he put in your parents' dope, I'd bet the entire club it was stuffed with hellhound DNA."

I slid to the concrete in shock. My life just became a lot more complicated.

CHAPTER 14

I went home and attempted to sleep. In between short bouts of rest, I had nightmares of being chased by huge violent dogs with vampire teeth. Or there were scenes of myself attacking everyone I knew because my rage had gotten out of control. Now all those weird dreams and visions were making more sense.

At six a.m., I gave up on any further sleep and took a shower. I managed to take down half a smoothie before I lost my appetite again. I tried not to think about Kai as I drove back to the medical center. I needed good news. Something to help me see the light at the end of a very dismal tunnel.

When I walked into Mom's room, she was sitting up.

"Mom!" I ran to her side and hugged her.

"Hi, baby." Her voice was raspy. "Are you okay?"

I pulled back to look at her. "Am I okay? You're the one that's in the hospital. Are you okay?"

"I've been better." She smiled and pushed a strand of hair behind my ear. "You look tired. Are you taking care of yourself?"

"Yes." I grasped her hand. Now was not the time to get into any details of my situation. There'd be time to talk when she had her strength back.

"Where's Baxter?" I looked around the room.

"Baxter?" Mom frowned. "Why would Baxter be here?"

Oh no. She hadn't seen him yet.

"Miranda May Saunders. Why did you ask that?" Her tone was as stern as it could be, under the circumstances.

"Because he's back," I said.

She blinked several times. "That's impossible."

"It's not." Baxter's voice came from the doorway. He held a cup of coffee in his hand.

"When did you wake up?" I asked her.

She couldn't take her eyes off Baxter. "I'm not sure. It wasn't that long ago. I've been drifting in and out a bit." Her mouth popped open, and she tried to say more, but words failed her.

"I'm gonna let you two talk. You have a lot to catch up on. I need to find Dr. Underwood." I slipped out of the room and shut the door behind me. I wasn't sure I wanted to hear the conversation coming next. Mom would need to get her anger out before she calmed down enough to listen to him.

I walked to the lobby in time to see Dr. Underwood coming through the main entrance.

I ran up to him. "I'm so glad I caught you."

"Good morning, Miranda. What news do you have for me?"

"Mom's awake."

"That's great news. I'll go see her now." He started for the wing containing her room.

"There's more," I said quickly. "I know what Doc did to my parents."

He stopped. "Also great, talk to me on the way."

"Hellhound DNA. He did whatever crazy spell he did with hellhound DNA," I blurted out.

"That would explain some of the odd things they are experiencing. How did you learn this?"

I sighed. "Let's just say I learned it the hard way. I'm part hellhound."

He gave me a sideways glance. "Well, that's interesting."

"To say the least," I muttered.

"I'll give your mom another checkup, then we'll talk to Doc about reversing it."

"Do you think he'll remember?" I asked.

"I hope so." He took a deep breath, then pasted on a smile as he opened the door to my mom's room.

THE NEXT COUPLE of days were touch and go. Mom and Baxter were both getting experimental treatment. Liam, Savage, and I all donated blood, since it seemed the hellhound element was needed to strengthen their immune systems. The vampire genes were failing, thanks to the curse Doc had put on the drugs they'd stolen, and there were no healthy cells to replace them. Mom and Baxter were both regaining strength in small strides. It was encouraging, but they still had a long way to go, both physically and in their relationship. But I was starting to see Mom smile more when Baxter was around, and I had a feeling things between them were going to be just fine.

I'd also started to understand why Mom was as cautious as she was. She'd made a lot of decisions in her life that didn't turn out so well for her. She was terrified I'd go down that same path, so she'd overcompensated with rigid rules, hoping to protect me. But we were both learning a lot of lessons. I couldn't learn from her mistakes if she never told me about them. And she couldn't help me with problems I faced if I never confided in her.

On the scientific front, Doc was working under the supervision of Dr. Underwood and a few other Seelie fae who were tasked with making sure the nasty little man didn't make a misstep. Most of the time, all it took was the threat of a visit from me to keep him motivated. It was odd, but I was glad he was that scared of me. It was a comforting feeling knowing I had some control over something in this crazy situation.

I still hadn't heard from Kai. I tried to remind myself that no matter what else happened, we'd never agreed to anything more than a temporary arrangement. He'd said he cared. And he'd sure kissed me like someone with feelings for me. But the heat of the moment can make a person do funny things. Maybe that's all it was—fear, adrenaline, and the uncertainty of the future. I could see how that could be mistaken for love when everything was on the line.

I didn't call him either. You couldn't make someone love you, no matter how much you loved them. And if you could, that wouldn't be real love, would it?

I was ready to turn in for the night when there was a knock at my door. It was almost ten p.m., and I wasn't expecting anyone. Zoey had brought my missed homework over so I could prepare for school Monday, but that had been hours ago, and I was pretty sure we'd covered everything.

I opened the door to see the biggest bouquet of daisies that I was sure had ever existed. Kai poked his head from behind them. "Can I come in?"

I nodded and stepped aside.

He placed the flowers on a side table, and I noticed he had a couple other things in his hands. "I come bearing gifts."

"You didn't have to." I wasn't sure I wanted them.

"I know, but I'm a nice guy so . . . here they are." He smirked, but I didn't respond. "Are you okay?"

I shrugged.

"Are you mad at me?"

"No," I said. "I'm just . . . disappointed. I thought we were friends."

He cleared his throat. "I thought we were more than that."

"I was starting to believe that, too, but then you ran off when I needed you most." I walked to the living area and flopped down on the sofa.

He followed me over, placing the wrapped gifts on the coffee table. "Listen, I'm really sorry about that. I had to work some things out. Not things about you, but about me."

"You couldn't pick up the phone? Ask how I was doing?"

"I wanted to, so many times. But I was afraid if I heard your voice, I'd come running back to you. I knew I needed to figure things out before I spoke to you again."

"What was there to figure out, Kai?" The heartache of seeing him again, fearing he didn't feel as I did, was breaking me. "Did you need to see if there were better options for you than a vampire-hellhound hybrid?"

"No. God no. That's not it at all." He pulled one of my hands to his chest. "This heart may not technically beat, but it still belongs to you. I'm pretty sure it was yours the moment I saw you walk into the cafeteria on my first day of school."

"So you're not bothered by what you saw in the woods?"

"It surprised me at first, but no, it doesn't change anything." He raised my hand from his chest to his lips and kissed my palm.

"What took you two days to figure out?" I still didn't know what to think about his absence and silence.

He lowered our hands to his lap. "I had a talk with Liam after we dropped off Doc. He gave me some good advice. I needed time to reflect on the future." He looked me in the eyes. "Do you remember when we left Baxter's, and I told you that we needed to talk when this was all over?"

I nodded.

"This is that talk." He cleared his throat. "You once asked me if my plan was to live life without a plan. I told you I had one, but I had to wait for the important parts to fall into place." He took a deep breath. "You are the most important part. I had to make peace with myself that if I couldn't convince you to give me a chance, I was going to move away and never come back."

"Kai . . ."

He shook his head. "Let me finish. I honestly never thought I had a chance with you. Then I saw you in the club, and I worried about what would happen to you. When Liam asked about you, I blurted out we were dating. It was a great cover, but a part of me was really glad I had an excuse to be with you. To pretend you were mine, even if it wasn't real. I have to be honest. Things weren't quite as dire as I made them out to be. Liam isn't as much of a tyrant as it seems. We still shouldn't cross him, but . . . I wasn't one hundred percent honest. I wanted a reason to spend time with you." He chuckled. "The day you kissed me in my room. Wow. I thought I'd just become the luckiest guy in the world. But I didn't know if I was kissing the girl I'd always wanted, or the girl that just needed me to find her father."

I looked at my hand still clutched in his. "I'm not that good of an actress, Kai."

He bit his bottom lip and smiled. "I hoped that was the answer. I know you have to finish school, and there are a lot of things ahead that are uncertain. But I'll be here through all of it, if you want me. I'm willing to wait, if you need time. I'll quit the club, sell the motorcycle, get a job in an office—whatever it takes to take care of you. Because, so help me, I'm in love with you, Miranda. I have been for a long time. I've always wanted you, but I knew you deserved better than the Kai Reynolds everyone thought they knew. I wasn't sure I could really be myself and stay here. You've shown me I can." He took another deep breath. "But if you don't see a future for us, just say the word, and I'll stay out of your way. I'll let you find someone who will make you happy, and I'll move on."

"You make me happy. I'll admit I never thought I'd say that. And Zoey is gonna faint when I tell her, but it's true. You make me very happy."

He pulled me to him and kissed me.

"I don't know what the future holds for us, but I'm happy to give us a try."

He bounced off the sofa and stepped backwards. "Speaking of the future, you need to open my gifts."

I eyed him suspiciously. "Okay."

He handed me a small box with a bow on it.

I pulled the top off the box, and inside was a folded piece of paper. When I unfolded it, there were a bunch of scientific-looking scribbles on it. "I don't get it."

"It's the formula to the cure for your parents. Dr. Underwood figured it out. It's requiring some more DNA shenanigans that I don't understand, and probably more fae magic, but who cares. They're gonna be okay."

I jumped up and threw my arms around him as I released happy tears. "Oh, Kai, this is the best news ever!"

"I thought you'd like it." He kissed the top of my head.

I wiped my eyes. "So what's in this one?" I reached for the other package, but he snatched it away. "Uh, it's nothing."

Now I was getting suspicious. "Then why did you bring it? Wrapped."

"Well, it was kind of a gag gift. Something to make you laugh. I thought you'd be in a better mood when I got here." He cleared his throat. "I didn't realize how much I hurt you when I took off."

"I can take a joke. Hand it over." I placed my hand out, palm up.

"Are you sure?" He was wearing that smirk I now had a love-hate relationship with.

"Yes, I'm sure."

He handed me the package. I sat on the sofa and unwrapped it. For a moment I just stared at the contents of the box, then I slowly raised my eyes to his. "Seriously."

He was snickering. Like a ten-year-old boy.

"So this is how it's gonna be between us, huh?"

He was now in the throes of a full belly laugh. "C'mon, you gotta admit it's funny."

I grinned. "I will admit that." I stood and put the box of dog treats on the coffee table. "But you need to know that I am fully prepared to pay you back for this."

He wiped his eyes. "I deserve whatever you do to me. I just couldn't resist that."

I patted his cheek. "You just wait."

He pulled me against him and kissed me again. "For you, I'll wait forever."

I smiled as I thought about how shocked he'd be when he learned I'd decided to buy my own death machine, and that Liam had promised to teach me how to ride.

~

WE HOPE you enjoyed this story in the Havenwood Falls High series of novellas featuring a variety of supernatural creatures. The series is a collaborative effort by multiple authors. Each book is generally a stand-alone, so you can read them in any order, although some authors will be writing sequels to their own stories. Please be aware when you choose your next read.

Other books in the Young Adult Havenwood Falls High series:

Written in the Stars by Kallie Ross
Reawakened by Morgan Wylie
The Fall by Kristen Yard
Somewhere Within by Amy Hale
Awaken the Soul by Michele G. Miller
Bound by Shadows by Cameo Renae
Inamorata by Randi Cooley Wilson
Fata Morgana by E.J. Fechenda
Forever Emeline by Katie M. John
Reclamation by AnnaLisa Grant
Avenoir by Daniele Lanzarotta
Avenge the Heart by Michele G. Miller
Curse the Night by R.K. Ryals
Blood & Iron by Amy Hale
Shadows & Spells by Cameo Renae (October 2018)
Falling Deep by J.L. Weil (November 2018)

More books releasing on a monthly basis. Stay up to date at
www.HavenwoodFalls.com

Subscribe to our reader group and receive free stories and more!

ABOUT THE AUTHOR

Since childhood, best-selling and award-winning author Amy Hale has been creating exceptional stories that summon a whirlwind of emotions and inspiration unto the reader. She loves creating characters and worlds from nothing but her imagination and a few glasses of wine. Her love of the written word has not only resulted in her writing some of her readers' favorite adventures, but has also manifested itself in the form of book hoarding. She's convinced it's not a sickness.

She debuted her first fiction novel in 2015 after retiring from thirteen years of nonfiction writing for various online entities. For the last couple of decades, she's also carried the titles of Laundry Goddess, Chef, Butt Wiper, Soother of Temper Tantrums, and in more recent years, Moderator of Sarcastic Eyerolls and Sass. She resides in Illinois with her husband, as well as two grown children who claim they are never moving out. Regardless, they are the center of her universe, although her cat believes otherwise.

If she had any spare time, she'd love music, photography, watching Mystery Science Theater 3000 with her family, and long rides on the back of her husband's motorcycle.

Learn more at authoramyhale.com

ACKNOWLEDGMENTS

There are times when "Thank You" never seems to say enough. This is certainly one of those times. I dearly love and appreciate everyone who has devoted time and energy into helping me make Miranda and Kai's story come to life. Without the help and support of such an amazing team behind me, this book would have never seen the light of day.

Many thanks to God for His grace and granting me patience as I stumbled and cried and wanted to throw my laptop across the room. I went through some big life upheavals while working on this book. And while they were good changes, they really messed with my writing mojo. I had to learn a new process, and there were moments when I wondered if this story would ever happen. Thankfully, it all came together on time.

My husband is my rock, and without him, I would never have attempted writing fiction. So if you see him at a signing (he's pretty much always with me) be sure to tell him thank you for supporting me. His support is why you have this book in your hands today.

Many thanks to my Havenwood Falls Family! Love to Regina for the gorgeous cover! And to Kristie Cook and Liz Ferry for making the book look amazing on the inside, as well as making sure my words make sense to all of you. They make sense in my head, but they don't always come out on paper that way. Kristie and Liz have the fun job of steering me back on the right path when my mind starts to wander off without me.

Thanks to my Havenwood Falls siblings for loaning me their characters. I appreciate you allowing them to pop in now and then!

A huge hug goes out to my beta readers Ashley Longcrier, Amber Peterson, and Felicia Thorn. You ladies helped me work through the plot, and I appreciate it so much!

As always, thanks to you, dear reader. You are the reason we keep telling these extraordinary stories of a town we all wish we could live in. I hope these books help you all keep your own little piece of Havenwood Falls with you wherever you are.

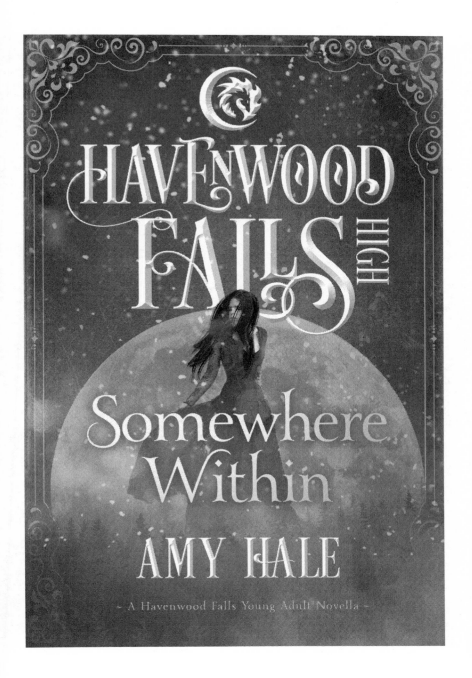

HAVENWOOD FALLS HIGH

Somewhere Within

AMY HALE

~ A Havenwood Falls Young Adult Novella ~

AN EXCERPT

Somewhere Within (A Havenwood Falls High Novella) by Amy Hale

With her raven-black hair, porcelain-white skin, and shy demeanor, Zoey Mills has been the target of bullies since childhood, no matter how many times her family moved. She expects nothing to change when they relocate to Havenwood Falls, her parents' hometown. What she doesn't expect is to discover that she inherited her eccentricities— as the next generation of a long line of frost dragons.

As she learns to accept she's on the cusp of becoming a shifter, she finds out her new best friend isn't human, either. But the boy Zoey's fallen for is, earning the disapproval of her grandfather and patriarch and fueling the fire of a decades-long feud among her extended family. Elitism and prejudice take on whole new meanings.

While she wants to trust her instincts and follow her heart, Zoey discovers that hiding who she really is and playing by the rules would make life a lot simpler. But simple doesn't mean easy. She must find her strength somewhere within and embrace her destiny—or risk losing everyone she cares about. And all of this on the eve of her Sweet Sixteen.

SOMEWHERE WITHIN

AN EXCERPT

I glanced at the boxes still waiting to be unpacked as I attempted to relax in my new bedroom. The excitement that generally accompanied a new house was missing. I felt like we moved more than we stayed still. My dad had assured me this would be the last time, and while I thought he believed that to be true, I had my reservations.

My first memories of moving took place at age seven. I don't remember all the details, but I do recall a loud commotion, after which Mom had run out to the backyard to get me. She rushed me into the car, and we left. Just like that. No goodbyes to the neighbors. No "grab a few things for overnight." We just left. Two days later, my dad arrived at our hotel room, two states away, driving a moving truck containing all our belongings. At the time, I was afraid to ask what happened, but it had certainly crossed my mind with every successive move. I'd had an unpleasant sensation down in my gut each time I attempted to mention the subject, so I'd always chickened out.

So there I was, on move . . . what was it? Move eight? Yeah, I thought this was move number eight. One would think I'd be used to starting over, and over, and over. But the truth was that with every packed box, I felt like I'd left a part of me behind. Even if that part wasn't important, it was a segment of my scattered life that no longer felt valid. Those memories now lived in the past.

This latest move had been prompted by a family member. It turned out I had a grandfather here in Havenwood Falls, Colorado. My parents had never talked about him before, so I'd assumed my dad didn't know who his father was. It was the only logical explanation for never hearing about Grandpa Mills. You couldn't talk about someone you didn't know, right?

My parents had received a letter that my grandfather, Lawrence Mills, had become very ill, and was possibly dying. Mom and Dad seemed frustrated by the phone conversations they'd had with him afterward. Ultimately, I held the impression they'd decided it was time to mend fences. Granted, they'd never told me what busted the fences to begin with, but maybe someday I'd learn all the deep, dirty family secrets. All families had a skeleton or two in their closets, so I'd heard. I suspected my family to be no different.

I stood and opened the box closest to my bed. It contained some of my clothes and the most beautiful jewelry box I'd ever seen. It'd been a gift from my parents for my sixteenth birthday. I hadn't actually had that birthday yet, but it was only about a month away. Dad had said that he wanted to give it to me before the move. "Something special for your new room," he'd said. I thought he'd been attempting to bribe me so I wouldn't complain about changing houses and schools yet again. It kinda worked.

I ran my fingers over the smooth metal casing, and I could almost feel it vibrate beneath my fingers. I didn't know how to explain it, but it felt as if the box itself was alive. Every time I touched it, I felt a zing of positive energy pulse through me. No doubt these sensations all took place in my mind, but I allowed myself to indulge the fantasy just the same. As long as I didn't say it out loud, I should be safe. Admitting it to others would have been like saying I'd grown a third leg, but no one could see it.

I placed the gold box on my nightstand and studied the intricate design on the lid, which looked much like a maze, with lines darting out from the center in odd geometric patterns. From the moment I laid eyes on it, I'd tried to figure out if there were some kind of labyrinth hidden in all the chaos, but if so, I had yet to solve it.

Regardless, it was another great addition to what my mother lovingly called my "jewelry hoard." I did have a slight obsession with jewelry, but really, what teenage girl didn't? I wouldn't call it a hoard.

"Zoey, here's another box with your name on it." Dad pushed through my bedroom door and set the box on the bed beside me. "Sheesh, that's heavy. What do you have in there? Anvils?"

I rolled my eyes at him. "Yes, Father. I have an anvil addiction. You've found me out."

He smirked. "So much sass in such a little person."

I reached over and pulled the tape from the top of the box, then glanced inside. "Oh," I said.

Dad simply raised his eyebrows in curiosity.

"It's my jewelry boxes," I said quietly.

His soft laughter followed him to the door, and he sent me a wink. "Enjoy." He walked out of the room and gently closed the door behind him.

I looked into the box again. I had several jewelry boxes, most of them very full. *Okay, maybe I do have a jewelry-hoarding issue. Is there a therapy for that?*

After lunch, Dad had some things to take care of at his new job running Simple Treasures Pawn Shop, so that left just Mom and me cleaning and unpacking in the kitchen.

Mom crossed her arms and leaned against the tan Formica counter. "What do you say we run into town for coffee? A latte sounds great, and I noticed a nice-looking shop as we drove through town."

I put away the last plate in the stack I'd unpacked and wiped my hands on my jeans. "Sure. Sounds good."

She smiled at me. "Perfect. As much as I love this new house, I'm eager to get out for a few minutes."

I didn't comment. I knew she wanted to hear me gush about the new place. After all, it was a nice house. A relatively new brick ranch house, it contained three bedrooms and loads of extra space. My bedroom easily overshadowed the dimensions of any other room I'd ever had. I even had my own bathroom. The pale yellow walls and white gauzy curtains gave my room a cheery feel. My white bedroom suite fit perfectly within the space. Much to my mother's delight, there were hardwood floors throughout. All I could think about was how cold those floors would be first thing in the morning. I made myself a mental note to ask for a rug in my bedroom.

The main part of the house had an open floor plan with the living room, kitchen, and dining room all in one large area. The fireplace had to be my favorite feature of the house, aside from my bedroom. The large grate could hold a decent-sized load of wood, and I could imagine the relaxing crackle as the flames warmed my fingers and toes while the smell of the fire saturated my clothes.

I had every reason to love our new home, yet all I could muster for my mother was a less-than-excited smile. As for the town—it was lovely. The gorgeous mountains surrounding the town boxed us in and lent a cozy, protected feel. As it was November, the air felt frigid and crisp, but also clean. Air this fresh was foreign to me, since all our other homes were in larger cities filled with smog and the various odors that accompanied living in a crowded area with several thousand people. One apartment had been so poorly located that a few times I wondered if I'd ever get the stench of garbage out of my nostrils. There was nothing like living a few blocks from a landfill when the wind blew just right. Thankfully, that stay was short-lived.

Havenwood Falls was perfectly sized for exploring. I hadn't had a chance to look everything over yet, but Mom assured me I could easily walk from one end of town to the other. Since I'd always felt pulled to the outdoors, I should have been thrilled, but moving and leaving what little stability we'd had dampened my spirits. The unknown was always scary. I'd never been good with change.

Mom pushed away from the counter. "C'mon, kiddo. Let's get some caffeine."

She wasn't kidding about the size of Havenwood Falls. We'd only been on the road a few minutes when we pulled into a spot in front of a collection of cute little storefronts on the town square. We stepped onto the sidewalk, and I glanced at the surrounding businesses. It seemed to be the typical small-town America kind of place, except for a few eclectic shops, which oddly didn't seem out of place. I spotted Madame Tahini's, whose sign advertised potions, palm readings, and other services. I couldn't say I'd ever been in a store like that. It intrigued me. It was at the end of the block, next to Simple Treasures Pawn Shop, which was owned by my grandfather and now managed by my dad.

Directly in front of our parking space was Coffee Haven. The bell over the door greeted us with the light tinkle of chimes as we entered the shop. The scent of coffee and baked goods hit me immediately. I was suddenly thankful for the distraction and the promise of chocolate. I wasn't as into the whole froufrou drink thing as my mom was. If it had a weird name and complicated list of ingredients, she'd try it. I honestly preferred hot cocoa over coffee. Thankfully, most coffee places offered both. With it being the first week in November, the weather was perfect for a warm drink.

I glanced around the cozy space, and my eyes were instantly drawn to a section near the back of the shop. Shiny silver, copper, and gold hung from various displays, and the overhead lights caused a sparkle from the beads and gems as I moved to the right or left. My quest for hot chocolate was all but forgotten.

"I see that look in your eye," Mom teased.

"What?" I shrugged. "I'm just looking around."

"Well, why don't you go look closer, and I'll order your drink. You want your usual? With peppermint?" She asked.

"Yeah, that'd be great. Thanks." I wasted no time in getting to the jewelry display. Several gorgeous pieces were front and center, and I couldn't help but reach out and touch them. I had an affinity for all jewelry, but these were expertly handcrafted by someone named Serena Alverson, and I found myself wishing I had such a creative gift. Of course, if I did, I'd likely end up with more jewelry than all the stores in town combined, so it was probably fortunate I didn't possess that talent.

I glanced down at the bracelet hanging from my wrist. It was my favorite, and my parents had gifted it to me on my tenth birthday. The green and yellow crystal beads were strung together on a delicate gold chain. Inside the gift box there had been a note indicating that the crystals were fluorite and yellow jasper, providing the dual function of an energy shield and a protective amulet. I wasn't sure I bought into all that, but I loved wearing it just the same.

"Zoey, here's your drink." My mom's voice pulled me from the allure of shiny objects, and she motioned for me to join her at a small table near the large picture window in front. My mother and I were opposites. Her short brown hair barely reached her shoulders, and her eye color matched it perfectly. Naturally petite, she possessed an inner grace and beauty. She preferred more casual clothing, but no matter what she wore, she made it look classy. She oozed charm and confidence. I did not. I was more comfortable reading in my room than I was socializing. Outside of us both having pale complexions and being short, I appeared to be nothing like her—a disappointing realization.

My dad was a tall man, easily over six feet in height with only a slightly darker skin tone and a muscular build. His hair had a thick texture with waves, and while dark, it was nowhere near the raven black of my own hair. His eyes were blue, where mine were gray with hints of blue. His self-assurance inspired me, and I had idolized him for as long as I could remember. He was my hero. I seemed so very different from them both. I often wondered if, upon my eighteenth birthday, they'd tell me I was adopted. It wouldn't have surprised me.

I took a seat opposite my mother and cupped the warm mug in my hands as I sipped it cautiously. Perfect. I looked up at the counter and noticed the young woman behind it smiling at me. Her name tag said Willow. *Such a pretty name!* I gave her a thumbs up to indicate my pleasure, and she winked at me, then turned to wipe down one of the espresso machines.

"So, what did you think of the jewelry? Anything you can't live without?" my mom asked as I took another careful sip of my drink.

"There are a few that are amazing, but I should probably at least get my room unpacked before I start adding more to my collection." I thought back to the various jewelry boxes in my room still waiting for my attention.

She laughed and reached across to pat my arm. Bad timing on her part, or on mine. As she moved, so did I—I scooted my mug to the side, directly in her path. Her fingers hit the cup and tipped it over, spilling the scalding hot contents all over my right hand.

I yelped in pain, and my mom jumped up to help me. Willow appeared at our side quickly, and I vaguely remembered hearing her ask how she could help. My instinct was to blow on the back of my hand, and to my amazement, impossibly cool air passed over my lips and cooled my skin. I watched in shock, and honestly some horror, as ice crystals formed over the burned area.

My mom wrapped her arms around me, shielding my hand and face from the view of those around us. A towel was thrust between our heads by a tight-smiled Willow.

"I've got this. Go take care of her before anyone notices." Willow's voice barely registered above a whisper.

She and my mom exchanged a look that I couldn't understand, then Mom nodded and ushered me out the door.

"It's okay, baby. Let's get you to the hospital to have that looked at." Mom spoke louder than necessary, and I began to think I was losing my mind—or dreaming.

The pain had disappeared, and I had a morbid eagerness to peek under the dish towel to see how bad my injury really was. I glanced back into the shop and saw Willow quickly cleaning up the mess we'd left behind.

It seemed like only seconds before I found myself sitting in the passenger seat as Mom backed out of her parking space.

I peeled the towel back from my hand, expecting to either see the worst, or see that I'd imagined the severe burn, but found nothing but a small mark. What I didn't expect to see . . . I didn't even know what it was. It was white, shimmery, and hard—almost like a shell.

Panic welled up in my chest. I struggled to breathe.

"Mom?" I could hear the fear in my own voice, so I knew she heard it too.

"It's okay, sweetheart. It's gonna be fine." She pulled out her cell phone and hit a button. "Call Tristan," she said loudly.

The phone answered back, "Calling Tristan Mills."

Mom put the phone to her ear and waited only a few seconds, then said, "Tristan, it's happening. Meet us at home as soon as you can."

I heard the muffled voice of my dad say, "On my way," and then the line went dead.

"Mom?" I asked again. "What is this? What's happening?"

She glanced at me and sighed a deep, worried-sounding breath. "It's a long story. Dad and I will explain it all when we get home."

We drove in silence until we reached our new house—not the hospital, by the way. My gut told me something big loomed before me. Something I was totally unprepared for.